WHERE WAS I BEING LED?

Amanda, or someone who wanted me to think she was Amanda, waited in the murky light at the far end of the yard. I stood listening to the toy's twinkling song.

Mary had a little lamb, little lamb...

She seemed to know where she was going and marched resolutely ahead, a silent little specter, allowing me to get no closer than following distance. When she ducked out of sight behind some trees, I thought I had lost her, until I heard the haunting song once again. Had she led my cousin on the same twilight quest?

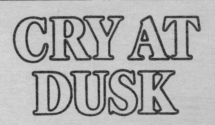

CRY AT DUSK

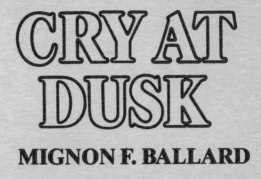

CRY AT DUSK

MIGNON F. BALLARD

WORLDWIDE®

TORONTO · NEW YORK · LONDON · PARIS
AMSTERDAM · STOCKHOLM · HAMBURG
ATHENS · MILAN · TOKYO · SYDNEY

CRY AT DUSK

A Worldwide Mystery/June 1989

First published by Dodd, Mead & Company, Inc.

ISBN 0-373-26025-3

For my sister, Sue Marie F. Lewis

ONE

I FELT AS IF she were with me and ached because she wasn't. Laney. My cousin, my classmate, my closest friend. People spoke our names in one breath: Laura and Laney, Laney and Laura, like bacon and eggs, bourbon and water. I was the water, Laney the bourbon. Hers was the spirit that gave life zest, and now she was gone. Dead.

My secondhand car hit a pothole in the road, and Vesuvius, my year-old black Labrador, yawned and broke wind in the back seat. I rolled down the window a few more inches and took a deep breath. Laney, then a senior in veterinary school, had given me the puppy already named. "Why Vesuvius?" I asked. "You'll find out," she said.

And I did. I smiled as we climbed the last hill before home. Laney could still make me laugh, even from beyond the grave. I could imagine her beside me, sitting in the passenger seat, bare feet on the dashboard, toenails painted a garish pink. Her straight blond hair would be flying across her face, smoke from her cigarette trailing out the window. Laney smoked too much, loved too freely, and wasn't afraid of the devil himself. The word *moderation* was not in her vocabulary.

My cousin's death in March three months before had left me wounded, bleeding, as if someone had ripped out part of my anatomy. I was incomplete. Her battered body washed ashore a few miles downstream from Crybaby Bridge on the Enoree River near her home. An open bottle of Scotch and one used glass were found on her kitchen counter.

An accident, they said. No one mentioned suicide, although I'm sure they considered it a possibility, and certainly no one suggested murder. Why would anyone want to kill Laney? I'm sure they must have wondered what she was doing alone on Crybaby Bridge in the middle of the night, a bizarre situation even for someone as impulsive as Laney McCall. But I knew something was wrong, and after three months of plaguing misgivings, I was determined to find some answers.

When my cousin was ten, her father had had too much to drink at a New Year's party and missed a curve on Harper's Hill. Both her parents were killed. After she had cried away all her tears, Laney swore she'd never touch alcohol, and as long as I knew her she never did. The Laney I knew was an experienced swimmer who respected water, and I knew she would never intentionally jump from Crybaby Bridge into the rain-swollen waters of the Enoree unless she meant to end her life. But was she the Laney I knew?

Crybaby Bridge. The thought of it made my stomach knot and my hands tremble. Set on a lonely stretch of boggy land, the wooden one-lane bridge was a favorite place for hayrides and parking couples. Around campfires' brave red flames, local campers tell the story of the young mother who walked onto the bridge on a grim, moonless night and threw her infant into the waters. On certain nights you can hear the baby crying, see its tiny form being swept beneath the bridge in an eddy of fog.

A folk tale, a silly ghost story that had been around for years, our Aunt Nell said. But where did it get its start, and why?

I had felt an aversion to the bridge even in bright daylight, but at night my apprehension grew. It wasn't the ghost story that bothered me as much as the aura of the bridge itself. There was something repugnant about it, something malignant, as though it had an influence of its own. I never wanted to see it again.

A FEW MILES from my hometown the road descended into a gentle valley with peach orchards on either side; trees were weighted down with the yellow ripening fruit we would enjoy all summer. It was a long drive across part of two states from where I now lived and worked in Atlanta, and I was glad to be home.

I slowed at the top of the hill and watched the road unwind like a silver snake in the night. The little town was asleep. The steeple of the Methodist church towered against the clouds. A fat, squatty water tank welcomed everyone to Redpath, South Carolina, home of the Redpath High School Fighting Warriors and the Long Red Line, its award-winning marching band. I smiled. Once long ago I had been a part of that Long Red Line, twirling my flag with the best of them while Laney cheered on the team with crimson pompoms, her ponytail flapping.

Now, like a silhouette from a nursery rhyme, the silent village slept, etched golden and black against a starry June sky. The sweet, heavy scent of magnolias welcomed me home.

"Will you walk into my parlor?" said the spider to the *fly....* Somewhere, in all this singsong innocence, a murderer faced each tomorrow as an uneasy challenge. Someone in our hometown had led my cousin too far over that delicate line between fact and fantasy, and that person was

just as responsible for her death as if he had pushed her off that bridge.

And it all began with an old log cabin and a phantom named Amanda.

TWO

"LAURA, I'VE JUST DISCOVERED the most fascinating place," Laney said when she came back to Redpath the first of the year. "It's an old cabin, I mean really old, stuck 'way back in the woods behind that house I've rented. Nobody has lived in it for years, and it looks like it's been there forever! I can't wait for you to see it."

Laney had surprised everyone when she decided to come home and go into practice with Bill Ratteree, our local vet. She had worked part time for Doc Ratteree since her high school days, and he was greatly responsible for her being accepted to veterinary school, but my cousin had always said she would never come back to Redpath to live.

And then there was Will, Laney's two-year-old son, a tiny replica of his mother with large intelligent brown eyes and a mouth so quick to smile, it made my heart hurt. If she had ever been married to the child's father, Laney wasn't telling, and most people didn't ask. I did, of course, and so did our Aunt Nell, who had raised her.

Laney just smiled that secret little smile of hers and mumbled something about ships that pass in the night. "Don't worry," she said, "he comes from good stock."

Aunt Nell took a deep breath and turned red in the face. "Seems to me like your two ships did a lot more than pass, and as far as I'm concerned, people from good stock don't have fatherless babies!"

"Of course he has a father," Laney assured us in her smooth, unruffled voice. "Did you think he was a clone?"

Maybe Will wasn't a clone, I thought, but his father was conveniently nonexistent. The baby went by his mother's name, McCall, and as far as I know, Laney neither expected nor received child support.

How like my cousin to defy convention by bringing her child home to raise in the town she had once jokingly called "Conformityville," and how like her to get away with it! It was almost as if she were daring them to talk, and maybe they did, but at least they had the good sense not to say anything around Aunt Nell or me.

My mother and Laney's mother were sisters, and we were born within a month of each other. We were raised in the same town, attended the same school, and were both well above average in height, but that's where the similarity ended. My dark hair curled around my face (with no encouragement from me), while Laney's buttercup yellow pageboy fell straight to her shoulders. My cousin excelled in sports, studied only when necessary, and was so involved in living, she had little time for sitting still; while I enjoyed music, was a fairly serious student, and honestly didn't mind staying at home once in a while with a good book. Until Laney went away to veterinary school and I to teach in Georgia after our graduation from college, we had been together all our lives, and I thought I knew my cousin better than anyone. I was now learning this wasn't true.

Laney had rented a small house on the outskirts of town where she could be close to her work, and she enrolled Will in a day-care center nearby. They had only been there a few weeks when she told me about the cabin. It was the kind of thing that would snare Laney's interest because it was shrouded in mystery as well as history, and my cousin was entranced by the unknown.

"Handhewn logs a foot thick," she said, "and this huge stone fireplace! The man who owns it thinks it was built before the War Between the States. He wants to give it to the Historical Society, but right now they can't afford to move it." I heard her fingers tapping the phone. "If I had the money," she said, "I'd buy it myself."

I groaned. Laney was off on another cause.

And then she found the locket, Amanda's locket.

"It's old, Laura, and dented and dirty, but it's gold, and there's something sort of sad about it. When I hold it, I want to cry." My cousin paused, and I thought she was going to indulge in a spell of tears as she sometimes did when she became emotionally wrapped up in something. But she took a deep breath and went on. "I found it behind a cupboard in that old cabin. It was wedged between a wall and the floor, and it has a name on it—Amanda!"

At first I thought Laney was merely curious, and so was I. Just who was this Amanda? When did she live there, and why did she leave her locket behind? But gradually she became almost obsessed with the subject.

It worried Aunt Nell. "It's on her mind all the time," she told me. "You know how she gets, Laura. This crazy Amanda thing has consumed her, and she *says* things, strange things." My aunt made funny little impatient noises. After thirty years of teaching fourth graders, she was accustomed to meeting problems head on, but she didn't know how to deal with this. "It's not right," she said. "I wish she'd never rented that place out there in the middle of nowhere!"

I smiled. Our aunt was getting older, more set in her ways, and I knew she wanted Laney and Will to move in with her; she was just too stubborn to admit it. Besides, Laney was—well, Laney. She could expand a dab of intrigue into a demanding, complex riddle. It was her way of life, and my cousin's life was never boring.

But when I talked with Laney over the phone a few days before she died, I wondered if Aunt Nell might have reason to be concerned.

"Tell me I'm not losing my marbles, Laura"—my cousin spoke in a whisper, as if she were reluctant to confide in me—"but sometimes I think she's here. I keep hearing this music...."

"Who's there? What music?" I was grading papers and wasn't in any mood for Laney's games.

"Amanda, of course! I told you about the locket, remember?"

"Yes," I said. "But why is Amanda so important? It seems to me you're making an awfully big deal out of this. If that locket belonged to Amanda and it's as old as you say, then she must have been dead for years."

"That's just it—oh, you'll never believe me. Look, I'm not sure yet who she is, but I'm going to find out!" My cousin hesitated. I could picture her sitting on her tiny living-room floor gnawing on a fingernail. "You're coming to the class reunion, aren't you?" she asked finally.

"Are you kidding? I'm counting the days until I can get as far as possible from Benjamin Smithfield Junior High!" I hadn't seen some of our classmates in the ten years since we had graduated, and I was eager to see who was losing their hair, who was losing their figure, and who was or wasn't losing their mate. But the reunion was in June, over three months away, I reminded her.

Laney groaned. "Can't you come any sooner, Laura?"

I sighed. It was time for my practical cousin routine. "I doubt it," I said, "and whatever you're up to with this Amanda thing, just forget it, Laney! I don't like the sound of it."

She laughed. It was a quick, high little giggle that meant, I'm going to do what I want whether you like it or not. I had heard it before. "Oh, come on, Laura, I can't stop now! There's something I have to find out, something about Amanda. I'll tell you all about it when you come."

"Like what? Tell me."

"I said *when you come*, Laura." I knew she was smiling, enjoying her teasing game.

"Laney, please." I was getting almost as nervous as Aunt Nell, and Laney knew it. She was laughing when she hung up.

Three nights later, unable to reach my cousin by phone, I called my aunt and told her of my fears. Laney had left a message about meeting Amanda at Crybaby Bridge. She had found a note, she said; Amanda needed her help. I had been out of town at a teachers' workshop and didn't get in until late. When I heard the message, I was frantic. I was also too late.

Life was going to be unbearably dull without her, and I resented her dying, resented that whimsical part of her that had let it happen, the part I could not share.

I drove through the dark streets of Redpath and pulled into the driveway of my aunt's quiet house. The porch light burned, and I could see Aunt Nell nodding in front of the television with her needlework in her lap. Little Will would be asleep in the small back room that had been his mother's.

Oh, Laney, why didn't you listen? I pressed trembling fingers against my temples and sat for a minute breathing deeply, calmly. It wouldn't do for my aunt to see me upset. Then I prodded my sleeping dog awake and hauled my luggage out of the trunk. Amanda, whoever or whatever she was, could wait until tomorrow.

THREE

"SO, WHAT'S-HIS-NAME isn't coming for the reunion," my aunt said the next morning at breakfast.

She knew very well what his name was. I had been dating Spencer Gaines off and on for the three years I'd been teaching at Benjamin Smithfield Junior High, but the two of them had never met. Actually, it wasn't Spencer's fault; I had never invited him to Redpath. This time I did; I needed his company, someone to hold my hand.

But Spencer wouldn't come. "This is something you'll have to do by yourself, Laura," he said. "It's your grief, go home and deal with it. Put it behind you." He kissed me lightly. "I'll be here when you get back."

He was taking a chance, and he knew it. I knew it, too. As a guidance counselor, Spence knew all about emotional dependency, and he wasn't having any of it, not from me. I loved him for that. But not enough, not yet.

As I was taking advantage of my visit to have my car repaired after a minor accident, I expected to stay in Redpath for several weeks. The old jalopy needed a paint job as well as a few essential replacement parts, and I had been putting off having it done.

Sausage sputtered in the cast-iron pan, and Aunt Nell lifted brown patties to drain. "You say he loves you, he sounds dependable, and there's nothing wrong with his looks, judging from that picture you showed me." She waved a spatula. "So what's wrong with the man?"

I laughed. "Nothing, really. And you'll meet him soon, I promise."

She turned back to the stove. "Clark Gable's dead, Laura, been dead for years. Besides, they say he really wasn't all that bright."

"But he sure was one hell of a man!" I said, momentarily forgetting my small cousin's presence. "Whoops! Sorry, Will!" I tied a bib around his neck and kissed his smooth baby cheek for the third time that morning. He looked like a Campbell's Soup commercial, sitting there in his high chair, all energy and good health. He had almost forgotten he had a mother.

"How long do you think you'll be able to stay?" My aunt avoided my eyes as she put a platter of eggs on the table. I knew she was fighting back tears.

"Oh, as long as it takes to get my old rattletrap fixed up," I answered lightly, "and as long as you'll put up with me. I've used Sam Dexter's garage before, and I know I can trust him."

With a high-pitched buzz, I made swooping airplane maneuvers around Will's head with a piece of buttered toast, and he shrieked with pleasure, clapping his sticky hands.

Aunt Nell set coffee in front of me. "You're welcome to stay all summer, you know that, and you can use Laney's car while you're here; I'm glad I didn't sell it now. It's good to have you home, Laura."

I squeezed her arm briefly, and made some silly comment about her big breakfast ruining my diet for the class reunion. Eventually we would have to talk about Laney, but not now, not in front of Will.

Aunt Nell and Uncle Tate had never had children of their own, and since her parents' death, Laney had been like a daughter to them. After Uncle Tate died three years ago, Aunt Nell had come to rely even more on Laney, and like me, she was having a difficult time dealing with her grief. When I came up for the funeral, I seriously doubted if she would be emotionally able to take care of Will, but I could see a remarkable improvement since then and knew the child was responsible for it.

Laney's place at the table was glaringly empty, and I put the platter there to keep it from looking so bare. I half-expected to see my cousin wander in, puffy-eyed, in that long purple T-shirt she slept in and sink groaning into the chair beside me.

My aunt must have been reading my mind. "She wasn't a morning person, was she? Had to drink about a pot of coffee just to open her eyes."

I nodded. "And at ten o'clock at night, when I was ready for bed, Laney was just getting started." After rooming together our freshman year in college, my cousin and I had agreed to remain friends by making other living arrangements. Laney never put the cap on the toothpaste, squeezed the tube in the middle, and left her clothes all over the floor; and I know I irritated her with my early rising and regimented neatness.

The bite of toast was like a sponge in my throat, and something was making my eyes water. It wasn't the coffee. My world was changing, and I didn't like it. It still seemed like Mom and Dad should be just down the street, I thought as we cleared away the dishes. My parents had moved to Virginia when Dad went with a new company during my junior year in college, and of course I visited them there, but Virginia wasn't home. Redpath was home, Redpath and Aunt Nell.

My aunt was strangely silent that morning, and once when the phone rang, she almost trampled me to answer it, then slammed down the receiver. "I've been getting some crank calls," she explained. "If a strange man phones, don't talk to him."

I asked her how I was going to know he was a strange man if I didn't talk to him, but she didn't explain. Later that morning we sat side by side in the old cane-bottom chairs on her latticed back porch while Will played happily in his sandbox. I had a feeling akin to déjà vu as the two of us sat there, leisurely stringing a mess of beans from a heaping market basket between us. The familiar snap of the beans and the thud as we threw them in the pan comforted me. A mound of curly green strings grew in the newspaper in my lap. I knew my aunt wanted to talk and was having trouble finding the words, but I didn't know how to help her.

"Laura," she said finally, "something is wrong. Something's bad wrong." She spoke in a hoarse whisper, never taking her eyes from her work. "The locket Laney found in that old cabin, and the little girl, Amanda, she talked about so much..." Her voice quivered. "Maybe you'll think I'm crazy, but if Laney hadn't found the locket, I believe she might be alive today. Tell me, do you think she really went to meet somebody on the bridge, or was she...imagining things?"

I felt my throat tighten. I didn't want to burden Aunt Nell with doubts, but I had questions, too, and it was natural for her to want to get to the bottom of things. "What was the police report?" I asked. I had put off asking because I dreaded hearing the answer, but it was something I had to know.

She finished stringing the handful of beans in her lap before answering. "Drowned," she whispered, glancing up at Will, "among other things; there were rocks, you know."

My head felt as heavy as stone. I should never have come back so soon; I wasn't ready to deal with this. "If only I had come home earlier that night," I said. "If I had called you sooner, we might have saved her."

"Hush! You called me as soon as you could. There was nothing we could have done."

"She tried to get me to come here, but I put her off, Aunt Nell. I told her she was carrying this Amanda thing too far, and then when she left that message about finding a note, I knew something was wrong."

My aunt shook her head. "I don't understand it; they never found that note—of course it could have gone in the river, too. Why would somebody do a thing like that to Laney?"

"I don't know," I said. "And what about that bottle of Scotch they found in her kitchen? Laney didn't drink. Anyone who knew her knows that."

She sighed and shoved a strand of hair from her face. "We don't *know* anything, Laura, especially about Laney. We may have thought we did, but Laney was a private person. There were things about her we may never find out, or even want to," she added. Her voice softened as she looked at Will, and she searched in her apron pocket for a tissue.

"I'll bet Will would like some peach ice cream," I said, eyeing the old hand-turned freezer that always sat on the porch. "And we should put him up a rope swing, too, on that same oak tree where Laney had hers."

Aunt Nell laughed. It wasn't much of a laugh, but it was the closest I'd seen her come to it since Laney died, and it made me smile to see it.

"I'll bet Laura would like some peach ice cream, too," she said. "And just who's going to tie this swing up into that great, tall tree? Or have you recovered from your fear of heights?"

I hadn't thought of that. "I'll find somebody," I told her. I remembered watching in fear as Uncle Tate inched out onto the large, sturdy limb to put up a swing for Laney and me. As badly as I wanted the swing, I was terrified that he might fall. The thought of climbing the tree made me weak. Unlike me, my cousin Laney had shimmied up, swung from, or walked across everything climbable in Redpath and the surrounding county. She wasn't even afraid of Crybaby Bridge.

I had never forgotten that long-ago summer day of the Bible school picnic when I was six. Our teacher took us on a nature hike over Crybaby Bridge, and Bobby Jack Culpepper chased me with a dead snake on a stick, forcing me against the metal framework so that I had to look either at the snake or at the rushing water far below. Laney had come to my rescue and knocked the snake away, but she wasn't above teasing me about my fear of heights. I stood suddenly, gathering the bean strings into a ball of newspaper, and walked to the end of the porch. It hurt to breathe.

"Laura, is anything wrong?" My aunt came and stood beside me.

I shook my head. Was anything right? Would it ever be right? "Cramp in my leg," I said finally.

She didn't believe me, of course. "Laura? You don't suppose Laney really meant to..." My aunt put her hand over her mouth as if to stop the words, the unspeakable words.

"No, I don't," I said softly. "That's not like Laney, not the Laney I knew."

She looked at me oddly. "Which Laney did you know? The one I knew behaved very strangely, heard ghostly music, and communicated with the dead."

"Is that what she told you?" I wiped my forehead with the back of my hand. It was barely midmorning, and the heat was stifling. "Did she really think she saw Amanda?"

"She saw someone she thought was Amanda," my aunt said firmly, "or she imagined she did. And that locket she supposedly found—well, I never saw it. I've searched that place over and I can't find it anywhere." She turned to take the beans into the kitchen. "I wonder if it ever existed."

"Don't worry," I said, "if it does, I'll find it." There were things about my cousin I might never know, but I was familiar with her hiding places, and I knew just where to look—if only someone else hadn't looked there first. But one way or another, I meant to find out what was going on.

FOUR

IT WAS OBVIOUS that someone had been in Laney's house besides Aunt Nell, and whoever it was had been looking for something. No furniture had been overturned, nor were the contents of drawers dumped out, and if I didn't know my aunt well, I might not have noticed it at all. There were little things: a dresser drawer not quite shut, a shirt sleeve caught in the crack of the closet door; the top was off of a china trinket jar my cousin kept by her bed, and the corner of a rug was turned up as if someone had left in a hurry.

The oil painting hung somewhat crookedly above a worn tweed sofa, and I knew that if the locket was still around, it would be hidden behind it, and it was. I found it dangling from the hook that held up the massive picture. A vivid seascape of rocky cliffs, turbulent waves, and dark storm clouds, it had always threatened me, made me dizzy to look at it, but it was a favorite of Laney's. Our grandmother had painted the canvas in college; it had belonged to Laney's mother and was one of the few things of hers she kept.

When we were in high school Laney concealed forbidden cigarettes in the recess behind the painting and, later on, love letters that she felt might shock our rather conventional aunt.

The small rented house was not much to look at, inside or out. A five-room brick veneer with a single carport, it stood a few yards from the road in a stand of scruffy pines, and with its picture window that took up most of one liv-

ing-room wall, it looked pretty much like a million others
built in the fifties. Less than a mile away was the river
where Laney died.

The few pieces of furniture Laney owned were still there.
A Mr. Riley who owned the bungalow planned to have it
painted before renting it in the fall, Aunt Nell explained,
and was in no hurry for her to remove my cousin's meager
belongings. "And a good thing," my aunt had added. "I
just don't think I can go in there again, not yet."

But she had been there earlier, probably with a caval-
cade of her friends armed with soapsuds and mops, because the house was clean, and I was sure Laney hadn't left
it that way.

I took the locket outside and sat on the small front
stoop, where I could examine it in the light.

So Amanda had really existed. Part of me had wanted
to believe that and part of me hadn't. The small oval locket
was warm in my hands and looked as if someone had at-
tempted to polish it. The locket was engraved with Amanda's name in flowing script, but who was Amanda?
Probably some far-removed kin of the Rileys who owned
the small house and the cabin behind it.

As Laney had described it, the locket was badly dented
and the catch was crushed. I used a nail file to pry it open,
expecting to find a faded photograph on the inside, but
there was nothing but the name *Lee*, followed by what
looked like the initial *C* or *G* and a date: *Oct. 8, 1935*.

Who in the world was Lee? Laney had never mentioned
him (or her?). Knowing my cousin's curiosity, I was sure
she had looked inside the locket.

I shoved the gold trinket in the pocket of my shorts and
tramped through dusty weeds around to the back of the
house, where parallel ruts of an old road cut deep into the

red soil. I followed it to the top of the hill, where the trail became barely discernible through high grass and erosion.

A crumbling stone chimney poked above sweet gum tops. A rusty tin roof tilted over ancient timbers. Fodder was stacked on the sagging porch, and wisteria clung to the crude gray walls. I felt as if I were looking into yesterday. And then a twig cracked above me, and a squirrel chattered on a limb over my head. This was his territory, his and Amanda's, and I was invading it. Whose territory had my cousin invaded?

I hurried through knee-high Queen Anne's lace back to the cottage, eager to get away. The heat of the small house was unbearable after the coolness of the woods. I would come back one night soon and collect the things of Laney's that my aunt wanted to give away. My cousin and I were the same size and often traded clothes; in fact, she had been wearing a favorite turquoise sweater of mine when she died, but I never wanted to see Laney's clothes again. They were too much a part of her, and I couldn't bear the reminder.

The tiny kitchen, although musty, was neat and clean. Laney wouldn't know it. I remembered the January night after I helped her move in; Will stayed overnight with Aunt Nell, and Laney and I sat at her kitchen table gorging on cold pizza. We giggled and gossiped until far into the night, and I felt closer to my cousin than I had in a long time.

The drapes were closed in Laney's room, and I yanked them open to let in the light. The room smelled faintly of tobacco, and I caught a slight whiff of her perfume—a secret, woodsy smell that reminded me of hidden springs, cool green ferns, and Laney, of course, and I knew I couldn't linger here.

I patted my pocket to be sure the locket was there and closed the door behind me. I would have to start at the beginning, as Laney had, to find out about Amanda. Surely one of the Rileys would remember her or could refer me to someone who might, but no one was at home when I lurched into the driveway of the farmhouse down the road in Laney's ancient orange Volkswagen. I had left my own car at the garage in town and was having a little difficulty adapting to a straight shift. When no one answered my knock, I remembered that Aunt Nell had said both of the Rileys worked at the carpet mill in town. I would have to talk with them later.

"I don't believe they've owned that land very long," my aunt said later that day as I sat on the back steps turning the crank on the ice cream churn. "I think all that property used to belong to the Squires. It backs up to their land." She pulled off her glasses in order to see to thread the needle for the bright cross-stitch pillow she was doing for Will's room.

"Well, at least we know there really was an Amanda," I said. I had shown my aunt the locket and put it away in my dresser drawer.

"Yes, and that's all we know: someone named Amanda once owned a gold locket; Laney could've invented the rest. For all we know, she bought that locket at a flea market!" She jabbed the needle into the circle of cloth and jerked at the thread.

"Aunt Nell, you don't really believe that, do you?" My arm was numb from cranking, and I shook my hand to get the feeling back. My aunt bustled inside for an answer and let the screen door slam behind her. I heard her lift the lid off the pot on the stove, where string beans simmered with streak o' lean and small new potatoes. It smelled like home, and my stomach growled hungrily.

Little Will shrieked as he and Vesuvius ran through the sprinkler in the backyard, and suddenly, as if their leader had lowered a baton, a chorus of July flies began their repetitious twilight song. It was strange how life went on.

Aunt Nell looked tired after supper, so I bathed Will and put him to bed, loving every minute of it. She was getting too old for the demands of childrearing, and I couldn't help but notice how she watched Will every minute, as if he might dissolve. I would be happy to assume the responsibility for the little boy who had become so much a part of my life, but I dared not mention the subject yet.

The wicker swing creaked as I joined her on the porch and the air was filled with the sweet scent of her red climbing roses.

"If anyone can tell you about Amanda, it would be Miss Annie Potts." Her voice came out of the darkness, and I glanced at her silhouette against a distant street light. A tall, robust woman, Aunt Nell seemed to have shrunk since my cousin's death, not only in stature but in demeanor. I sat in the rocker and put my feet on the porch railing, hoping she would tell me to take them down, but she didn't.

"How is Miss Annie?" I asked. "She must be at least a hundred and ten!" The woman had taught me in the third grade, and I had thought she was ancient then.

"I expect she's somewhere in her late seventies, and she still cuts her own lawn, for your information!" My aunt paused for that to sink in. "But years ago Miss Annie taught in a little county school out near where Laney lived. It was before they consolidated; Loganwood, I think it was called. Annie Potts knew just about everyone in that part of the county, and not much happened that she didn't know about."

Just then, Vesuvius, who was stretched across the top step, made a very rude noise and shifted his position.

"I've been meaning to talk to you about that dog, Laura," my aunt said. "I believe he has a problem; do you think maybe we should change his diet?" I could hear her apron flapping as she fanned herself in the darkness, and I began to laugh, silently at first, and then the sounds rolled out in loud gasps until I thought I would never stop. My aunt laughed, too, and I reached out and found her hand. She pulled me into the swing beside her, and the two of us sat there for a long time crying quietly together.

FIVE

MISS ANNIE POTTS added a splash of crimson to her painting and jammed the paintbrush into a glass of brownish water. She was painting a still life of zinnias in a blue pitcher. This was the third one she had started since my visit began, and each got progressively worse.

"Scoggins, their name was, Maxie and Jasper Scoggins. The woman was as broad as a barn and wouldn't know a bar of soap if you bopped her over the head with it; and that sorry husband of hers never hit a lick at a snake! Must've had seven or eight kids: little pale, stringy-haired stairsteps."

Since Miss Annie couldn't hear well, she assumed no one else could either, and I jumped instinctively at her loud voice. "It's funny your asking me," she said. "Your cousin Laney came to me back in the winter wanting to know the same thing."

"It was because of this," I said. "Laney found it in that old cabin." I showed her the locket and the inscription inside. "Do you have any idea who Lee might have been?" I asked.

She frowned. "Well, I've known many a Lee, but I can't think of any who would figure in a relationship with this child." She smiled. "Amanda, now, would be hard to forget, and I remember her wearing this." She touched the locket with a paint-smeared finger. "Poor little thing! I always wondered how she came by it."

"What about the date?" I asked. "Can you tell me anything about that?"

Miss Annie waved the locket away. "You read it, my eyes aren't so good."

"October 8, 1935. Does that mean anything?"

"Probably her birth date," she said. "It would be about right." She made a yellow blob on the paper in a style Laney would say was reminiscent of Vincent van Gauche. I stifled a giggle. "Do you remember what she was like?"

"Oh yes, dainty little thing, not like the rest of them, and right smart, too." Bifocals slipped down her long nose as she frowned at her efforts. "That was back when we had several classes in one room; I had Amanda for first and second grades."

"And this would be about when? Early forties?" I tried not to wince as she dribbled huge drops of purple on the page.

"Let's see now." Miss Annie frowned. "That would be about forty-five, no, forty-four years ago. If Amanda Scoggins were alive now, she'd be fifty-two years old and probably as coarse and fat as her mama, although you'd never have thought so back then." Her voice boomed out at me. "Genes will tell, though, genes will tell."

"What do you mean, if she were alive?"

Miss Annie shook her head solemnly. "Drowned in the Enoree the summer before she turned eight—happened just below Crybaby Bridge. I'd gone back to school that summer to work on my certificate and didn't hear about it until I got home. Nobody seemed to know how it happened."

I shivered. "Crybaby Bridge! Is that where it got its name?"

"Oh, lord no, honey! That's been called Crybaby Bridge since way before I was born, before my mama was born. Who knows how it got its name; that old story probably has its roots in fact, but we'll never know."

"And you say the Scoggins family lived in that old cabin on the Rileys' property?" I asked.

"Yes, but it wasn't the Rileys' then. Homer Riley didn't have two nickels to rub together back then, and neither did his pa. All that land belonged to the Squires. Old Colonel Squires, the judge's father, was still alive then."

"I talked with Mr. Riley last night," I told her. "He said he bought that acreage about ten years ago and has never used the cabin for anything but storing hay."

"Humph! Well, the colonel rented it out for a long time after the Scogginses left. Squeeze a penny till Lincoln screamed, that man would, and the judge is just like him!" She wiped her hands on a color-splotched rag. "Ada, now, she was different. Ada was Judge Decatur Squires's younger sister," she added. "A pretty girl, and the children just loved her. Sometimes she'd fill in for me at school, spoiled them rotten of course, but I always thought she should have been a teacher. She died though, right young." Miss Annie blew on her wet painting. "Rheumatic fever. Ada never was strong." She pressed the picture into my hands. "Here, you take this. Give it to your Aunt Nell, bless her heart. I can paint another."

The soggy picture rode home on the seat beside me. So Amanda had died as a child, and she had drowned in the Enoree, like Laney. A hint of a chill ran through me, and I decided not to tell my aunt how the child had died, at least not for a while.

Aunt Nell looked up smiling as I came into the kitchen where Will was making glue out of a peanut butter and jelly sandwich. "You've had two phone calls," she said. "Ginny Adair's expecting you this afternoon to help make sandwiches for the class picnic tomorrow." She offered Will a swallow of milk from his Miss Piggy cup. "And what's-his-name wants you to call him back."

I kissed her flushed cheek, noticing the fine lines around her eyes and the strands of graying brown hair clinging to her damp forehead. "Sit down, and I'll fix us some iced tea and a sandwich," I told her. "I'll call Spencer after lunch."

I laid Miss Annie's vivid painting on the kitchen table. "I brought you a present," I said, "painted just this morning. She wanted you to have it."

"Oh...well, that's sweet of her, isn't it?" My aunt looked at the damp picture from several angles. "Where do you think I should put it?"

I stared silently at the trash can.

Aunt Nell laughed. "Laura, you're awful! You're getting as bad as—"

"As bad as Laney?" I tossed ice into glasses. "It's all right, I don't mind being compared to Laney; in fact, I'm kind of flattered."

She stirred sugar into her tea. "What did you find out about Amanda?"

"She was a child of some tenants who lived in the old cabin back when it belonged to the Squires." I concentrated on spreading tuna salad on whole wheat bread.

"And?" My aunt removed Will's disgusting bib and threw it into the sink.

"And...she died. That's all."

Will screamed at having his face and hands washed and tried to wiggle out of his chair. "How?" My aunt persisted. "How did she die?"

"She drowned," I said. "Aunt Nell, this happened almost fifty years ago. It had nothing to do with us or with Laney."

"I'll bet Daisy Leatherwood would remember her, or maybe Nevin or Delia Squires," she said, lifting Will to freedom. "They were all raised out there, and they would be about the same age. Judge Decatur Squires brought up the three children when his wife died, shortly after Delia was born."

It always came as a shock to me to be reminded that plump, aggressive Daisy Leatherwood, who had presided over almost every club and chaired numerous committees in Redpath since I could remember, was a sibling of the frail, soft-spoken Nevin Squires and their shy sister Delia.

Mr. Nevin Squires had been the librarian at the county library for as long as I could remember, and because of his expert guidance, he was responsible for many a passing grade on high school term papers. He and Miss Delia, both in their fifties, had never married, and they lived with their father, the judge, on the old family farm, Willowbend, on the Enoree River.

Their older sister, Daisy Leatherwood, presided over her husband, a wealthy Realtor, and two cocker spaniels in a spacious house in town, and her son Austin was a high school classmate and one-time boyfriend of Laney's. The two of them had dated steadily their senior year in high school, but my cousin broke off the relationship when they went away to college. "It's a big ocean out there," she said to me, "and I don't intend to jump in with an anchor around my neck." I hoped she had explained this in gentler terms to Austin, but I doubted it.

"Laura," my aunt said suddenly, "you don't suppose Austin Leatherwood had anything to do with—" She glanced at Will, who was rummaging happily in the trash can, and sighed.

"Let me!" I washed his hands for the second time and sent him into the backyard with a cookie. "If you want my opinion, for what it's worth, Austin would never harm Laney," I said. "He was hurt when she broke off with

him, and angry, but he loved her, Aunt Nell. I think he always will."

My aunt stacked dishes in the sink. "I'm being silly, I
know, but...well, they had been seeing one another again;
just as friends, Laney said, but then, you never know."
She wiped damp hands on her apron. "Daisy Leatherwood would've had a hissy fit if she'd thought they were
getting serious again. She never did like Laney."

I laughed. "Laney didn't think too much of her, either.
She called her 'Snakehole Mouth,' remember? We used to
make fun of her up there singing in the choir."

Aunt Nell swiped at the table with a soapy rag. "I never
saw a woman with a name that suited her less—Daisy.
Huh!"

"Maybe I'll get a chance to ask about Amanda tomorrow," I said. "They're having our class picnic out at Willowbend, you know."

"If you have time, you might drop by the library on
your way to Ginny's this afternoon," she said. "I have
some books about overdue, and it will give you an excuse
to talk to Nevin.

"But before you go, before Will goes down for his nap,
how about playing something for me? Do you get a chance
to practice the piano at all?" She shooed me into the living room. "I miss hearing you play."

I played some of her favorites. Aunt Nell liked the old
songs, nostalgic tunes popular in the early part of the century. She said they made her feel safe and happy.

"You still have a nice touch," she said. "I always
thought you should have majored in music, Laura."

I smiled. "You're prejudiced. I'm afraid I wouldn't have
gotten very far—too much competition."

"Are you afraid of competition?"

Her question jolted me. "Well, no, but one has to face the facts, and unfortunately, I don't think I had the talent or the stamina."

She jerked off her glasses and stuffed them into her pocket. "I don't know where in the world you got that idea!"

I shrugged and was in the middle of "In the Good Old Summertime" when Will came in tired and crying because he had scraped his knee. After a glass of juice and several renditions of "The Billy Goats Gruff," I finally got him down for his nap and returned Spencer's call. It was good to hear his voice.

"I just want to be sure you don't forget me," he said. "Is everything all right?" He sounded a little guilty for letting me go it alone, and it served him right to worry, I thought.

"We're okay," I whispered. "And Spence, there really was an Amanda and a locket. I found it. Laney didn't make it up after all."

"Laura, you know your cousin was sort of inclined to flights of fancy. Don't you start!"

"Don't be so clinical," I said. "I'm just trying to find out who she was. Amanda was a flesh-and-blood child, and she died like Laney—in the Enoree River!"

"I can be there after lunch tomorrow," he said after a pause.

I laughed. "Spence, you'd be bored to death! Old home week at Redpath High, and you wouldn't know a soul. I'll do you a favor and pass on that offer."

"Are you sure you're okay?" Maybe it was my imagination, but he sounded relieved.

"I'm fine," I assured him, "and I'm late. I'm supposed to be at a friend's making sandwiches right now."

"Laura, wait!" Spencer spoke slowly, measuring his words. "I've always thought Laney's death was an accident or, God forbid, maybe even suicide.... I still think so, but you will be careful, won't you?"

"I will," I promised. But be careful of what? Careful of my aunt? My classmates? Careful of the people I had known all my life?

A year ago I would have laughed at the suggestion, but now I wasn't so sure.

SIX

"FOR GOODNESS' SAKE, take that dog with you," my aunt suggested as I started for Ginny's. "If he doesn't need the air, I do!" And she laughed at her own joke. She watched from the front steps as we started down the walk. "Laura, you will be on the lookout for strangers, won't you? Redpath isn't the same little town it used to be, so do be careful."

I promised, but I didn't understand. What did my aunt mean, Redpath wasn't the same? It seemed familiar to me. Since I had been home, I had walked the same streets and spoken to the same people who lived in the same houses they had always lived in. What was different about it? And who was Aunt Nell afraid of? Just after lunch she had hurried to answer the phone, and later, when I noticed the receiver was off the hook, she explained that she didn't want anyone waking Will from his nap. It was a plausible excuse; why couldn't I accept it?

Since the Adairs lived only a few blocks away, I decided to walk. Both Vesuvius and I could use the exercise, but because it was the hottest part of the day, we followed the coolest route, walking under the line of oaks that shaded Redpath's oldest residential streets. We passed the prim white Presbyterian church where Laney and I went to Sunday school and sang in the junior choir, and where my cousin had turned loose a jar of lightning bugs during the candlelight service when Miss Reenie Ramsey, our Sunday school teacher, got married. Miss Reenie never had much to do with Laney after that.

On the opposite corner was the gray stone Baptist
church where we went to Bible school every summer. My
cousin went because they always served Eskimo Pies for
refreshments, and I went because Laney went.

Vesuvius tugged at his leash to hurry me along, but I
held him back as we turned down Academy Street. The old
red-brick grammar school that had seemed to swallow me
up as a child looked smaller now, dwarfed by ancient syc-
amores that splashed the deserted playground in shadow.
Once when Laney had made a D on her report card, she
had climbed to the top of one and hidden there, crouched
on a limb until it was almost dark. Aunt Nell and Uncle
Tate were so relieved to have her safely down, they for-
gave her for the bad spelling grade.

I rested on the low brick wall that surrounded the
grounds. The earth was hard and bare where we had
played in the building's shade, and I wondered if children
still jumped rope there.

I closed my eyes, seeing Laney, skirttail flying, skip-
ping to the old familiar rhyme:

> *Last night and the night before,*
> *A lemon and a pickle came a knockin' at my door.*
> *I opened the door to let them in,*
> *They hit me on the head with a rolling pin!*

She could jump "hot pepper" up to one hundred without missing. As nimble-footed as a ballet dancer, my
cousin would never have fallen from Crybaby Bridge.
Anyone who grew up with Laney would be aware of this.
Surely my Aunt Nell had thought of it. Did the police
know it, too?

I traced the rough mortar between the bricks, a part of
yesterday, a part of today, and that gnawing emptiness of

losing Laney began in my chest and worked its way to my head, to my stomach, with tentacles of grief. I would have to get used to Redpath without her.

Vesuvius, straining after a skittering squirrel, pulled me to my feet, and I put the school and its memories behind me, for a while at least, and hurried down the street to the library. I was curious to find out if Mr. Nevin Squires remembered the child Amanda and the circumstances of her death. According to Miss Annie Potts, the little girl had been dead for over forty years, yet she had a strange hold on my cousin, and I wanted to know why.

Nevin Squires smiled at me from behind a stack of books and held out his hand. "Well now, it's Laura Graham! Back for the reunion, I'll bet. It's good to see you again." His hand was small and slender, but the grip was strong, and his smile sincere. I wanted to kiss his cheek but was afraid it might embarrass him.

"You always make coming to the library seem like coming home," I said, returning my aunt's two books. I smiled, thinking of all the hours I had spent there gathering facts for my senior English paper on Edna St. Vincent Millay. The library had been a peaceful retreat in those otherwise-hectic high school days, and it hadn't changed. A few people browsed in the tall stacks, their feet moving quietly over the cool green carpet. Mr. Sam Peterson, who clerked at the post office, read the morning paper at one of the glossy oak tables while resting his feet. He greeted me with a nod and a smile and turned to the sports section.

Mr. Nevin Squires looked like a dapper Spencer Tracy in hornrimmed glasses, and he always wore a flower in his buttonhole. Today it was a blue sweet William. Laney had said he kept *Playboy* magazines behind his desk and read them when he thought no one was looking, but I never knew if it was true.

I tried not to think of this as he led me to a group of armchairs by the window. "I'm glad you came in today, Laura. I've been wanting to tell you how sorry I am about your cousin." He perched on the edge of the chair beside me and slowly patted the arm of mine as if my hand were there. "That was a terrible, terrible thing. I can't seem to get it off my mind." He removed his glasses and rubbed the bridge of his nose. "And your Aunt Nell, how is she?"

"Looking after Will doesn't leave her much time to grieve," I said. "It's a good thing she retired last year. A two-year-old is a full-time job."

"Well now, for someone your aunt's age it is." He studied me solemnly with myopic brown eyes. "When are you coming home, Laura? Your aunt needs you."

"I know," I said, "and we'll work it out; it just takes time." I almost smiled. If I had been a man, I doubted that he would have even considered asking me to give up my job and my life style and hurry back home. In spite of his gentle ways, my old friend was a bit of a chauvinist.

"By the way," I said, taking advantage of the pause, "do you remember a little girl named Amanda who used to live in that old cabin on your place?"

He made a show of putting on his glasses. Was he avoiding my eyes? "The cabin! Why, we haven't rented that old place in years. Don't even own it anymore."

"I know," I said, "but this was years ago, back when Miss Annie Potts taught out at Loganwood School. She had Amanda in her class for a couple of years, and I thought you might remember her. Didn't you and your sisters go there, too?"

He nodded, frowning. "Amanda . . . yes . . . she was Delia's age. Rather pretty child, not like the rest." Nevin

Squires drew in his lips as if he smelled something bad. "She was one of that Scoggins brood, all common as pig tracks except for her. Amanda didn't seem to belong."

"Do you remember what happened to her?" I kept an eye on the front desk, hoping no one would disturb us.

"I believe she died." He stared at a hunting print on the wall. "Grandpa had words with old Jasper Scoggins, Amanda's daddy, and the family moved away. We never saw any of them again."

He started to rise, but I put a delaying hand on his arm. "You don't remember how she died?"

"Laura, you forget, that was almost fifty years ago! I was only a child myself." He chuckled softly. "Why do you want to know?"

I explained about the locket. "Laney seemed to think it was important," I told him, "and there's an inscription on the inside giving her birth date and the name Lee. Do you have any idea who that could be?"

"Well now, I believe she may have had an older sister by that name." He made a steeple of his fingers. "However, I can't imagine any of the Scoggins lot being able to buy a gold locket. Why, some of them even went without shoes!"

"I'm surprised Laney didn't ask you about Amanda," I said. "Miss Annie said she had come to her, and I'm afraid I'm making a nuisance of myself trailing along after her asking the same questions."

He nodded at Mr. Peterson as he left. "She may have tried, but I was in the hospital for a few weeks back in the winter." He held up a hand to ward off my concern. "Nothing major."

"Oh, I see," I said. "Well, I'm not sure how much she learned, but I thought I'd try and find out what I could. I think Laney would want me to."

He took both my hands in his and gave them a gentle squeeze. "Laney is gone now, Laura. I know you loved your cousin, but you have other people to think of now, beginning with Laura Graham."

He meant well, I know, but his words struck a sensitive nerve, and I wanted to cry out what I had not yet put into words: *Laura Graham doesn't exist, shouldn't exist, until I find out what happened to Laney!*

I woke Vesuvius, who slept in the shade of a boxwood beside the library door, and continued down the street to Ginny's. Was the summer heat steaming my mind, or was Nevin Squires trying to give me a kindly warning?

SEVEN

"BUDDY CALLAHAN'S COMING." Ginny smeared a slice of bread with pimento cheese and drained the lemonade from her glass. The rattle of ice cubes gave the illusion of coolness, but the kitchen was warm in spite of the air conditioning. "He divorced last year, you know, so watch out! He'll be trying to make up for lost time."

I cut a stack of sandwiches into neat triangles. "Oh, lord! to think I actually dated *that*!"

"Well, that was before the beer gut and the red Corvette. Vroom-vroom!" Ginny giggled. "Actually, Buddy wasn't bad looking in high school, and let's face it, Laura, we wouldn't have had much of a football team without him."

"I guess you're right," I said, "but we're not seventeen anymore, thank goodness!" I smiled. It had been kind of fun dating Buddy my last year in high school. He was a good dancer and a popular football player, and I think he might have even been a little bit in love with me, which is flattering at any age. We often got together for picnics and swimming with Laney and Austin Leatherwood and usually ended up necking on Aunt Nell's cozy dark front porch.

"This is the last of the cheese spread, thank goodness!" Ginny put the empty bowl in the sink and stood to stretch. "We had some good times back then, Laura. Remember those parties you and Laney gave?" Her happy expression faded, and she busied herself scooping bread crusts into a freezer bag. We had spent an afternoon spreading three hundred pieces of bread with chicken salad and pimento cheese, and she had until now avoided mentioning Laney's name.

"How could I forget?" I said. "Laney's whole life was a party. She knew how to make living fun." I tucked my last sandwich into the box and grabbed a paper towel. Tears again! Would they ever stop?

"Laura, I'm sorry." Ginny put her hand on my shoulder. "I shouldn't have said...this must be terrible for you. I don't see how you stand it." Now Ginny was crying, too. She had grown up with Laney and me and was always a good friend. In fact, both of us were bridesmaids when Ginny married her high school sweetheart, Larry Adair.

"I have to face it sometime. It might as well be now," I said. I watched the crumbs disappear as Ginny swirled a sponge over the table. If Laney were here, we would be laughing, not just talking about it. My cousin was a woman of action. "Let's have a party," she would say, and would immediately begin phoning people. Or, "There's a double-feature horror movie playing in Columbia. Let's get up a bunch and take it in." "Don't wait too long at the fair" was Laney's advice to anyone she thought life was passing by.

Laney had not just given life a try; she had joyfully immersed herself in it, unaware of its dangerous, hidden currents. It was still hard for me to believe that she wasn't coming back, that we would be celebrating our high school reunion without her.

"Tell me again who's coming tomorrow," I said as Ginny and I rewarded ourselves with cold beer on the patio. Vesuvius had given up exploring the fenced-in backyard and was trying to make friends with the Adair family cat, who would have none of him.

"Well, Austin, naturally, since the picnic will be at their old homeplace, and Blakely Floyd, of course." Ginny flipped up her sunglasses to squint at me. "Can you believe she's still after Austin? That woman just never gives up! And of course, Mama Daisy's all for it."

"Maybe she'll catch him now that Laney's gone," I said. "At least she deserves credit for trying. Should we award her some sort of certificate?"

"Laura, you're awful! Austin Leatherwood doesn't care two hoots and a holler about Blakely Floyd." Ginny held the cool glass against her cheek and sighed. "She should've married that podiatrist from Greenville when she had the chance."

"I guess it's kinda hard to get romantic about somebody who's examined your feet," I said.

"Remember how she used to get mad and go home when she didn't get her way when we were little?" Ginny asked. "Well, she hasn't had her way lately with much of anything. Those last two business ventures were flops, and I don't think her love life is faring much better."

"Maybe we can match her up with Junior Pittman. Is he coming?"

Ginny nodded, laughing silently, and sat up abruptly in her lounge chair. "You sound just like Laney! Poor Blakely, she's really an attractive woman, and she wears good-looking clothes. She just went after the wrong man. Austin never loved anyone but Laney." She shoved her chair into the shade. "It's funny you should mention Junior. He's coming—why, I don't know—and by himself, of course. Remember when he asked every girl in the junior class to the prom and still couldn't get a date?"

"I remember. I think I was somewhere in the middle of the list. He asked Laney the day before, and she told him to get lost. I thought it was kind of brave of him just to call her."

Ginny frowned. "Laney could be cruel sometimes, but I don't think she ever meant to be. It really hurt Austin when she gave him back his class ring."

"Aunt Nell said she was seeing him again."

"I saw them with Will getting hamburgers one night, and they sat behind us at the senior play," Ginny said. "It gave me the strangest feeling, like looking into the past."

"Do you think they were more than friends?" I asked.

She shrugged. "I don't know, I just remember thinking, 'I hope she doesn't hurt him again.'" Ginny held the cat on her lap and stroked its fur. "Laura, don't take this wrong; I know you were close to Laney, but, well, you'll have to admit she was different. Like the little boy, Will. She just expected us to accept him with no questions asked, and the funny thing is, most of us did."

The cat spat at Vesuvius, who came to sit at our feet, and darted behind a dogwood tree. "Sometimes your cousin did peculiar things," she said, "things I didn't understand." She rubbed Vesuvius between his ears. "I liked her, liked her a lot, but I never could figure her out."

"Ginny, did Laney ever mention Amanda to you?" I asked.

She frowned. "Amanda? No, I don't think so. I only saw her a few times after she came back home, and we never had a chance to talk. Why? Who's Amanda?"

"It's a long story," I said. "I think I'd better have another beer."

"Better still, stay for supper. The girls are spending the weekend with their grandmother, and Larry won't be home until late. Come on, Laura! Let's go wild and order a pizza, pretend we're eighteen again!" She made a face.

"Or we could have pimento cheese and chicken salad sandwiches."

I laughed. Ginny still looked like a college girl in spite of being the mother of four-year-old twins, and as chairman of the reunion committee, she had worked hard planning this weekend. "I'll pass on the sandwiches, just the same, but the pizza sounds great," I said. "Just let me call Aunt Nell so she won't expect me."

While we sat on the patio eating our pizza, I told Ginny about finding Amanda's locket and how my cousin had become almost possessed by the enigma of a child who had died years before.

"You say the little girl drowned?" Ginny asked, tossing Vesuvius a slice of pepperoni.

"I think so. No one seems to be sure, but I mean to find out, for Laney's sake if for no other reason. The night Laney died, she said she'd had a note from Amanda asking her to meet her at the bridge."

"Surely she wasn't serious!" Ginny looked at me. "You don't believe that, do you?"

"I don't know what to believe," I said. "Maybe I'll learn something about Amanda tomorrow at Willowbend. I'm sure Austin's mother remembers her. She's the oldest, isn't she?"

"Daisy Leatherwood! I've never known that woman to do anything unless there was something in it for her."

"Maybe Austin will ask her for me," I said. "He's not like his mother, thank goodness!"

Ginny sat suddenly forward, nostrils twitching. "My God!" she said. "Ugh!" and jumped up to fan herself with a paper plate.

Vesuvius had performed his usual feat, not without pride. Head high, he seemed to smile.

"Is that your dog?" Ginny gasped, eyes round with horror. She started to laugh. "I'm sorry, Laura, but he does have a problem. Where on earth did you get him?"

"Guess," I said. I knew it was time to go. "It's past time for his supper," I explained. "I fed him before we came, but he's a big dog."

"He certainly is," Ginny said with both hands over her face. "Listen, I'll drive you home if you're afraid to walk.... We can roll down the windows. I don't mind, really."

"Thanks, but I don't mind walking, and it will give us a chance to...clear the air." We clung weakly together laughing as Ginny walked with me to the gate. She wiped her eyes on her shirttail. "Laney makes us laugh even when she's not here," she said.

Ginny paused with her hand on the fence. She wasn't laughing now. "Laura, what if somebody did leave a note that night asking Laney to meet them? Not Amanda, of course, I don't believe in ghosts; but someone else, some-one living. Someone who didn't want her to know how Amanda died."

No one passed me as I walked home on the silent streets, and I was glad to have my big dog with me even in his present condition. Ginny's last words stayed in my mind: *Laura, I think you'd better be careful. Forget Amanda, forget her!*

It was the third warning I'd had that day, and it was be-ginning to irritate me, like a commercial repeated too fre-quently: *Don't settle for second best.... Don't suffer from the discomfort of... Don't be embarrassed by...don't...don't...don't!*

I cut through the park, passed the small gazebo band-stand where the Long Red Line had often played for pep rallies and where the old men of Redpath sat on sunny mornings to discuss world affairs, and stopped for Vesuvius to sniff at a tree. The bandstand was a favorite landmark of mine. Red geraniums in hanging baskets swayed from its scalloped eaves, and roses bloomed around the worn brick foundations. I had stooped to sniff a blossom when I heard someone approaching from the other side of the small building.

The dim streetlamps did little to illuminate the darkness, and I wasn't naive enough to believe that bad things happen only in cities. A woman alone had no business in the park at ten o'clock at night, dog or no dog. Vesuvius had decided to nose in the other direction, and I yanked on his leash and walked faster, deliberately forsaking the paved walks for the quiet, cushioned grass.

Feeling my way from tree to tree, I climbed over the waist-high stone wall and dropped to the ground on the other side. Vesuvius frolicked along beside me, thinking it was a great game. Across the street the deserted schoolyard looked like an etching in the moonlight. I stopped in the shadows and heard nothing but the barking of a distant dog and the hum of a faraway car whose headlights were like cat's eyes in the night. No footsteps.

"Come on boy. We're almost home," I said aloud, feeling rather silly for my imagined fears. And then the footsteps began again, louder, faster than before, and my momentary braveness vanished.

I started to run. Vesuvius, sensing my fear, picked up speed, galloping well ahead of me. Some guard dog, I thought. If only he would turn and growl, threaten our pursuer, the stalker would probably run screaming in the other direction. But he didn't. Whoever was chasing us was getting closer, and I was out of breath.

EIGHT

THE HOUSE ON THE CORNER was dark. The family who lived there had either gone to bed or were out of town, but I could see a dim yellow light from the back of the house next door. Miss Emma Hightower was probably in the kitchen enjoying a late-night snack. Miss Emma was also as deaf as a disc jockey at a rock station; I could pound the door down before she'd hear my cries for help.

My heart was making such a noise, I thought it was going to conk out on me. And then I remembered the magnolia tree in the next block. Magnolias made wonderful hiding places with their dark foliage sweeping the ground like a tent. As children, Laney and I had hidden under this one many times while playing. Tonight I wasn't playing. I took a deep gulp of air and dashed down the street like an Olympic contender—only I wasn't an athlete and my side hurt with every breath. We were almost there and I started to slow down, but Vesuvius didn't want to stop. He liked running.

"Slow down, you fool dog, you'll get us both killed!" I whispered, digging in my heels. And then I dared to look behind me, and there he was, not quite a block away. He walked quickly and with determination, and I think he shouted something, but I didn't stop to listen.

I had my mouth open to scream when I saw the headlights, glorious yellow headlights, washing over the lonely black street. The car stopped beside me, and I had my hand on the door even before I knew who it was. I didn't care who it was. All I wanted to do was get in and get away—fast.

"For heaven's sake, why didn't you phone me, Laura? I would have picked you up at Ginny's," my Aunt Nell said.

I quickly shoved Vesuvius into the back seat and collapsed in the front. I was thankful for the darkness so my aunt couldn't see the relief on my face. My hands shook as I buckled my seatbelt, and as we pulled away I looked up to see the man who had been following me dart into the shadows.

"I remembered that you didn't take a car, and when I called Ginny to tell her I'd come for you, she told me you'd left." My aunt's voice took on its familiar classroom tone. "Sometimes I wonder if you young people have any sense at all, Laura! You shouldn't be out walking alone at night. Where in the world have you been, anyway? I've been riding all over town."

"I'm sorry. I took a short cut through the park," I said, trying to keep my voice even. I glanced in the seat behind me, where Vesuvius had stretched full length. "Where's Will?"

"Ann Thomas ran over to stay with him," she said. "It's a good thing I have an obliging next-door neighbor."

"I wasn't thinking," I said. "I should have let Ginny drive me home."

"Forget it. I'm a crabby old woman." She touched my hand gently. "I just get a little nervous, that's all, with these pesky phone calls. No one bothered you, did they?"

"Who's bothering you, Aunt Nell? Why won't you tell me? Have you told the police?"

"No, no, it's nothing more than a nuisance, someone I'd rather not talk with. I didn't mean to alarm you," she said in an offhand manner, and I knew I wasn't going to learn any more.

"I didn't come here to add to your worries," I said. "Believe it or not, I hoped to alleviate some of them." I was glad I hadn't told my aunt about being followed. "In fact," I said brightly, "I'll start tomorrow. The picnic at Willowbend is for children, too, so I thought I'd take Will along. How would you like the afternoon off?"

"But won't he be a lot of trouble? I mean, you don't want to be bothered with looking after Will, and there's that river so close by..."

"Aunt Nell, you're going to have to let him out of your sight sometime! They're going to have organized activities for the children, and he'll get to play with others his age. I promise he'll be fine." I tried to keep the aggravation from my voice. I couldn't blame my aunt for being protective, but it wasn't good for Will.

After some argument, I finally convinced her to let me take Will along, so the next day I dressed my small cousin in his blue sunsuit with an elephant on the front and, armed with a bag of diapers, a change of clothes and his plastic cup with a spout, set out for the old Squires home.

Willowbend had been built in the first part of the century from rough yellowish rocks that look as if they're permanently mudstained. Judge Decatur Squires's father, old Colonel Porter Squires, had built it to house his growing family, without regard for architectural appeal. Skirted by porches on three sides, it contained three stories and a full attic crowned by a grim-looking cupola, and it sat like a giant wart on the landscape. The head-high hedge surrounding it did little to soften its lines.

"The fortress of the frog king," Laney had called it. She'd loved to tease Austin about his family home. He accepted this good-naturedly, as he did her other jokes, by admitting the house was ugly, but he didn't have to live in it. In fact, he stayed away from it and from his grandfather, Judge Decatur Squires, as much as possible. That's why I was surprised to learn he had offered to have the class picnic there.

As soon as I arrived, I realized this was just another step in Daisy Leatherwood's master plan. Enthroned on a front-porch rocker, she regally greeted the adult guests while Blakely Floyd escorted the children to the backyard to play. Blakely's mother and Austin's had been close friends for years, and both would like nothing better than for their two children to marry. With Blakely's approval, they plotted constantly toward this goal.

A dainty pink Sunday-school princess still, Blakely Floyd looked the part of the docile, happy homemaker with her soft blond curls, large gray eyes, and expensive green sundress. She might as well have a little flower-shaped badge over her heart that read, "Goodness dwells herein." But I grew up with her, and I knew better.

Will cried and clung to my hand as she stooped, smiling, beside him. "Don't you want to play with the others, Will?" Blakely asked in her oozing honeyed voice. "There are swings and a slide. Do you like to seesaw?"

"Can you believe they still have Austin's old playground things back there?" she said to me. "Now I don't feel quite so old!"

Will sniffed and wrapped both arms around my leg. I hoped he would throw a temper fit and put Blakely in her place.

"How about a cookie?" she asked. *Cookie*—the magic word. Will abandoned the safety of my leg and trotted right after her, the little traitor.

Blakely smiled over her shoulder. "He'll be fine, Laura, don't worry. I have two baby-sitters watching them."

I managed a silent nod. It was the best I could do, and since there was no way I could avoid the old dragon on the porch, I dutifully climbed the steps to pay my respects.

Daisy Leatherwood extended a plump, freckled hand that glittered with two large diamonds and a sapphire. "Laura Graham!" She pulled me forward in a stout grasp. "Here, sit with me awhile and tell me about yourself. Are you still playing the piano? How's your Aunt Nell?"

I meekly accepted her invitation, a little surprised at my warm reception. Now that Laney was not there to threaten her precious son, she could afford to be nice to me. Someone shouted my name, and I waved in reply, yearning to join my classmates congregating on the lawn. "I—uh— promised Ginny I'd help set up tables," I said, inching out of my chair.

"Bosh! A few minutes longer won't hurt." She pushed me back with one hand. "Now, about your aunt.... How in the world is she going to raise a child at her age? Why, she's not much younger than I am! Why didn't you take the little boy, Laura?"

I found myself smiling. How like Daisy Leatherwood to get right to the point. "It may come to that," I said, "but right now she's satisfied, and so is Will, and I'd rather leave things as they are for a while."

"That Laney!" Daisy's many chins sagged as she shook her head. Her hair, tinted a reddish gold and set in rigid waves, resembled painted plaster on an old doll. Not a hair moved in the humid breeze. "She had no business bringing a fatherless child into the world, and now the poor little thing hasn't even a mother."

I felt anger bubbling like boiling water in my chest. The nerve of the woman! Silently, I gripped the arms of my chair.

"I'm sorry," she said. "I say too much sometimes. I know you loved Laney, and I'm sorry about what happened, sorry for all of you."

"Mrs. Leatherwood, did Laney ever ask you about Amanda?" I asked, remembering my mission.

Her eyes snapped shut, and she leaned back in her chair. "Amanda Scoggins? Yes, she did. Belonged to that lowlife family that lived in the old cabin. Trashy bunch! Papa wouldn't let us play with them." Her voice dropped so low, I had to strain to hear it. "Commonordinary," she whispered, "just commonordinary." I tried not to smile at the term. I had heard my aunt use it, too. It was the worst thing you could label a person in their vernacular.

"Do you remember how she died?" I asked.

She blinked at me like a sleepy cat. "Drowned, they said, right down there in the Enoree, and I wasn't surprised. That slob of a mother never knew where those children were. Never cared, I guess." Daisy Leatherwood sat forward in her chair. "Your cousin said she'd found a locket of hers, a gold locket now, in that old cabin!" She laughed without joy. "I told her it must have been somebody else's. It couldn't have belonged to a Scoggins."

Several classmates moved up to the porch to speak to their hostess, and I made my escape, disappointed that I hadn't learned anything new. Like her brother Nevin, she remembered Amanda having a sister named Lee or Leigh but had no idea what had happened to her.

Sometime during the picnic I would try to search out Miss Delia, Daisy's younger sister, who lived at Willowbend with her brother and father. Maybe I would be lucky enough to talk with the old man himself.

"Miss Delia's sweet, but she doesn't say much," Laney had said. "She just works in her rose garden and pastes things into her scrapbook, and cooks, of course." Even

Aunt Nell admitted that Delia Squires was by far the best cook in the county. The youngest of the judge's three off-spring, she had gone a few years to Winthrop College for Women, then came straight home to keep house for her father and brother. If she ever had a serious relationship with a man, I never heard about it, although according to Aunt Nell, Delia Squires had been a pretty young girl; even now, in her early fifties, her features were porcelain smooth and as delicate as a figurine's.

My classmates greeted me pleasantly, although there were some awkward pauses when they remembered that my life-long companion would not be coming. I guess it was a little like seeing Laurel without Hardy or Tweedledum without Tweedledee. I worked my way through the crowd and found Will being carried on the shoulders of a pretty teenage girl. With a cookie in his hand and chocolate on his face, he seemed to have forgotten I ever existed. I smiled at his unrestrained laughter, at his absolute joy in the moment.

"Just like his mother. 'Pleasure is the beginning and the end of living happily.'" Austin Leatherwood stood behind me, his hand on my shoulder.

"Says who?" I asked, returning his hug. I hadn't seen him since Laney's funeral, and there were still faint shadows under his eyes, but I noticed an ease about him that I had never seen before.

He smiled. "Says Epicurus. You should know; it was the quote under Laney's picture in our senior annual. You put it there yourself."

"That was a few years ago," I said, frowning as Will tried to push another child off the seesaw. Austin chuckled. "See, just like his mother!"

"He's two years old," I reminded him. Still, Will did look remarkably like Laney's baby pictures with his flaxen hair and large, mischievous eyes. His father had obviously been fair, too, and whoever he was, he wasn't Austin Leatherwood. A redheaded, freckle-faced terror of a child, Austin's freckles had faded, and his bright hair had darkened to a beautiful auburn.

"I want to talk with you later," Austin said as someone called his name. He looked at his watch. "Why not meet me at five on the kitchen porch? Nobody will bother us there."

I nodded. "Austin, where can I find your Aunt Delia? There's something I want to ask her."

"Aunt Delia? Who knows! She probably hid at the first hint of company. If she ventures out at all, she'll be in her rose garden."

I saw Ginny and Larry Adair unloading giant coolers from their station wagon and hurried to give them a hand, remembering my promise to help.

"Oh good, you're here!" Ginny stacked my arms with three large containers of fruit salad and sent me stumbling toward the kitchen. Suddenly my burden was reduced, and I could actually see where I was going as someone removed the top of my tottering load.

Red-faced and perspiring with beer in hand, Buddy Callahan, man of my dreams, grinned down at me. "Let me give you a hand, little lady," he said, tucking a plastic container under his moist arm.

Calling on all my inner sources of strength, I refrained from making a face. There were several more cartons of food to be moved, and we needed all the help we could get.

"That's all we can do for now," Ginny told me as I lingered in the kitchen. "You might as well get on out there and socialize, have a few beers. I'll call you when we're ready to serve."

I gave her a dirty look as Buddy waited eagerly beside me. Some friend she turned out to be! I let Buddy lead me to the shade of a gnarled dogwood, where we sipped cold beer and reminisced. The shade was welcome, the beer refreshing, and the conversation boring. For twenty minutes or more I listened to the tale of Buddy's marital woes, his crooked business partner, and his shrewd bargaining in buying a very large boat, while his sweaty hand inched slowly around my shoulders and his puffy red face hovered close to mine.

Suddenly, in the heat of the moment, my beer slipped out of my hand, dousing my classmate's orange plaid polyester shorts with at least eight ounces of Milwaukee's finest.

I fled amid apologies, after having tried to remedy the situation with a bandanna dipped in the ice water in a washtub full of beer. With the temperature in the eighties, Buddy's shorts would soon be dry, but I hoped his ardor had cooled permanently.

Not many people were aware of Miss Delia Squires's rose garden, but I had gone there a few times in high school with Laney and Austin and knew of the narrow gap in the hedge that led through a latticed arbor to flower-bordered walks. The arbor was shady and cool, with wooden benches on either side, and the sweet scent of fragile pink climbing roses surrounded me.

I sighed as the gate clicked shut behind me, relieved to have escaped Buddy Callahan and pleased to have found this lovely, peaceful place. And then I noticed the slender young man sitting on the bench in the shadows and felt a slight feeling of misgiving as he stood and came toward me.

He had changed, but I still recognized his face. Junior Pittman. He reached out a narrow white hand. "I've been waiting for you," he said.

NINE

I MUST HAVE TURNED instinctively toward the gate, because he blocked me with one quick step. "Wait! Please don't go. I won't keep you long, I promise."

I didn't like his looks, and I didn't like him waiting for me there in the garden with no one else around. Buddy Callahan suddenly didn't seem so bad after all, but after what I'd done to him, would he come if I screamed? Probably not.

"I heard you earlier asking Austin where to find his aunt," he admitted, jamming his hands in his pockets. He wore Levi jeans: very new, very neat, and very hot. "I really wasn't trying to eavesdrop," Junior explained. "I was just coming up to talk to you, but you got away before I could get your attention." He smiled, and I noticed he had had his teeth capped. "Then I saw you dump that beer on old Callahan, and I knew you'd probably come in here to get away."

I laughed and sat down on the bench. "You won't tell, will you?"

He shrugged. "Who would I tell?" He sat abruptly on the seat across from me, propped his elbows on his knees, and rested his chin on his hands, looking for all the world like a praying mantis.

We sat there silently for a while, appraising each other. I noticed that he no longer wore glasses and that his acne had cleared up, but his Adam's apple was still as prominent as ever. I wondered if he noticed any improvements in me.

"So? Talk," I said finally.

"Look, I'm sorry about your cousin," he began, staring at a spot between his feet. "She wasn't very nice to me, and to tell you the truth I didn't like her, but I'm sorry she died." He looked up shyly. "I guess—I guess it must be pretty hard on you."

I nodded. "Why are you saying this to me, Junior?"

"Not Junior, please!" His face turned a shade paler, and he held up a hand, palm out. "I don't use that name anymore. Call me Rex."

If Laney had been there she would have said, "Okay. Here, Rex! Here, Rex!" I wasn't Laney, but the temptation was still there. I felt a giggle rising in my throat and pretended to scratch a bite on my leg so he wouldn't see my face.

"Somebody told me you lived in Atlanta," he said. "I've had a pretty good offer with an electronics firm there, and I just wanted to know how you liked it, and about the housing situation, the cost of living—that kind of thing."

"Oh," I said. "Well of course, I'll be glad to tell you what I can." It was easy to discuss impersonal things with Junior. He asked questions, and I answered them. While rose leaves moved feebly in tepid air and lacy shadows merged on the sandy path, we talked about apartments, and shopping malls and the price of food until I reminded him I had to meet Austin.

"Oh sure, I almost forgot." When he stood, his head almost touched the top of the bower. He turned toward the gate, then stopped. "You know, I thought you'd be a concert pianist by now."

I had a feeling I had let him down, that I should apologize.

He drew a line in the sand with his shoe. "By the way, are you going to the party tomorrow night?"

Was he asking me for a date? I swallowed. "By all means," I said, smiling in what I thought was a kindly way. "I promised Austin I'd be there early to help with name tags." I had promised Austin nothing of the kind, and for all I knew we weren't even using name tags, in which case I would just have to go out and buy some.

"Oh," he said, backing away. "Well, I guess I'll see you there, then."

"Sure," I said. Poor Junior! He was so accustomed to rejection, his response was automatic. "Rex . . . wait!" I called. "Save me a dance, okay?" I disliked myself for feeling so righteous. Was Blakely Floyd rubbing off on me?

I still had fifteen minutes before it was time to meet Austin, and in the heavy summer silence I heard the snipping of shears in a far corner of the garden where the path curved out of sight. Miss Delia's little patchwork world looked like a colored illustration from a child's nursery book. I wound my way through banks of fragrant sweet William, mounds of fuchsia impatiens, and clusters of white candytuft, past a simple blue enamel pan set on a stand as a birdbath. Roses of every variety bloomed on each side; I recognized a Peace, a Talisman, and a deep red that might be a Mr. Lincoln, and then I stopped counting.

I found Delia on the other side of a slender weeping willow, scooping grass clippings from a wheelbarrow onto a bed of pale pink sweetheart roses. In a bucket beside her stood an armful of the delicate flowers mixed with baby's breath and asparagus fern. She wore a blue cotton house dress with elbow-length sleeves and low-heeled gray oxfords. A tendril of brown hair escaped from under her floppy straw hat and wafted over her cheek. The instant she saw me, she froze, crouched there like a startled rabbit.

"I'm sorry, I didn't mean to frighten you," I said, introducing myself. "I'm a classmate of Austin's, and I remembered your lovely garden from high school days. I hope you don't mind the intrusion." I smiled. "It's beautiful here, Miss Delia. You must work out here constantly."

She dabbed at her moist face with a flower printed handkerchief and slowly pulled off bulky gloves. "You're Nell's niece, aren't you? The other one."

"I'm Laura. Laura Graham. I grew up here in Redpath, but I teach in Atlanta now."

She nodded solemnly. Her eyes were soft and brown and serious. She knew who I was now. I must have been looking at the cut flowers, because she reached out to the blossoms, barely touching their petals. "They're for the table," she said, "the picnic tonight."

"They're lovely," I said. "Can I carry them for you?" I noticed an open book face down on a bench under the willow. It looked cool and inviting there, and the sun was hot on my hatless head, but she didn't ask me to sit. She merely smiled and nodded as I picked up the bucket of flowers.

"Miss Delia," I began as we walked slowly down the twisting path, "do you remember my cousin Laney who lived near the old cabin?"

She stooped to clip another rose and added it to the others. "Oh yes, a bright butterfly of a girl." She touched my arm. "I'm sorry."

"Thank you." I watched her face as I spoke. She looked like a subject in an old painting with her flushed cheeks and downcast eyes. "She told me about Amanda," I said, "the child Amanda. Do you remember her, Miss Delia?"

She broke off a branch of bridal wreath spirea and held it to my nose. "Don't you love the scent? We used to dress up in Mama's old curtains and wind these around our heads and play bride...."

"Hm, reminds me of summer," I said. "Laney and I did that, too. But about Amanda," I reminded her.

"Yes, she wore a blue ribbon. Always a blue ribbon. Tiny little thing..."

"Your sister said she drowned in the Enoree," I said. "They found her below Crybaby Bridge. Do you remember how it happened, Miss Delia? She must have been close to your age."

"The bridge." She lost the color from her face; the pruning shears dangled from her hand. We had reached the arbor, and she sank onto the seat, her breath coming in short gasps.

Since there was nothing else to fan her with, I quickly removed her hat. Her color frightened me, but I was reluctant to leave her to go for help. "Are you all right, Miss Delia? Can I get you something? Water?"

Wordlessly she pointed to a hydrant on the other side of the trellis and pressed the balled-up handkerchief in my hand. After she held the wet cloth to her face, her breathing slowed, and color began to return.

I sat there on the bench beside her, feeling a little like a wilted flower myself. "Better now?" I asked.

She nodded. "Yes, much better, thank you."

"You scared me there for a minute," I confessed. "I'm sorry, maybe I shouldn't have asked you that. But my cousin Laney had kind of a wild imagination, and I'm trying to sort out fact from fiction."

She looked steadily at a spot across from her and smoothed back her hair with both hands. It was dark and glossy, with just a hint of red and was tied back from her face with a faded pink ribbon.

"Laney claimed she had heard some kind of music, that she had even seen Amanda." I laughed softly, trying to make light of the issue. "That couldn't be true, I know, but there was a locket, Amanda's locket, and it had an inscription in it. I thought since she lived so close, Laney might have mentioned it to you."

Delia Squires looked at me then. She looked at me as if she hadn't heard a word I'd said. "The flowers will wilt. We'd better get them inside," she said. A wall had come down around her, an invisible wall as unyielding as steel, and I knew I had touched the core of an old hurt.

As we rose to go, I heard footsteps on the other side of the gate. "Delia? Adelia, are you in there?" Nevin Squires stepped through the narrow opening and stopped short when he saw us standing there. "Well now, I thought I'd find you here, and there's Laura. I was going to offer my help with the flowers, but I can see you two don't need me."

He held the gate open for us, and Miss Delia scurried away. I was left to bring up the rear and the bucket of roses.

"Your sister gave me a scare," I told Nevin. "I asked her about Amanda and the way she died, and I thought she was going to faint."

"She hyperventilates," he explained. "Scared to death of water, and especially of that old bridge. Poor Delia, she can't even talk about it."

But why? I wondered. There had to be a reason. But I kept my thoughts to myself.

TEN

THE KITCHEN PORCH was empty except for an old picnic table with watermelon seeds in the cracks, berry-stained market baskets, and a couple of cane-bottom chairs. It was a few minutes after five, and Austin was nowhere in sight. I poked my head into the kitchen to see if Ginny could use my help, but there was no one there, either.

And then I heard a giggle, a shriek, and the sound of tiny feet running in the upstairs hall above me.

"Come back here, Gina!" a young voice said. "No, Will, *no*! Hey, now wait just a minute!"

I took the steps two at a time to find the teenage sitter, whose name I later discovered was Michelle, chasing down a hallway after a laughing toddler in training pants, who disappeared inside a room and slammed the door behind her.

"What happened?" I asked, turning the corner at full speed.

The poor kid looked as if she wished she'd never left home that day. "Gina wanted to use the bathroom, and Will needed a diaper change, so I brought them upstairs together." She jerked open the door at the end of the hall and looked frantically around. "Now they've gone in different directions, and Will doesn't have on a stitch!"

I laughed. "Where did he go?"

She pointed. "Upstairs, I think. Would you mind…?"

"I'll find him," I said, already on my way. I could see she had her hands full with Gina.

The house had no central air conditioning, although there were ceiling fans that kept the two lower floors relatively cool; but not a molecule of air stirred on the unused third story, which must have felt something like the devil's own waiting room. If Will had been foolish enough to come up here, he wouldn't stay long.

"Will," I called sweetly, "it's Laura! I'll bet you can't find me!" I pretended to hide behind a massive oak wardrobe and waited while sweat trickled down my face. "Will!" I yelled again, "Laura has cookies!" Still nothing. A fit of sneezing overtook me, but of course I had no tissues. And where was Austin when I needed him?

From the far end of the dim hallway I heard a low, childish laugh and the faint creaking of stairs. The attic! I had forgotten about the attic. I raced down the narrow passageway, knocking over an umbrella stand and backing into a glass-enclosed bookcase. Some other time (in January, perhaps) I would like to see what it contained. And then from somewhere above me I heard it, a familiar refrain from a childhood song played on a windup toy. I smiled. Will was teasing me, but I would find him now.

The attic stairs, enclosed on either side, were dark and empty, but the door swung open at the top, revealing a gray half-light. "Will? Honey, it's hot and dirty up there," I said. "Let's go down and get some nice cold ice cream." I stumbled on the steps and put out a hand to steady myself. I could feel the grime on my fingers; Will would have to be scrubbed from head to toe.

The attic smelled of time-scorched papers and musty, faded clothing. On a cool, rainy day it would make a wonderful place for children to play dress-up. The large square room with slanting ceilings was stacked with curious-looking boxes, humpback trunks, and abandoned furniture. I flicked on a dim light and prowled the room,

probing dark corners and perspiring profusely while my
patience drained and was replaced by anxiety. It was unlike a two-year-old to stay quiet and hidden this long,
especially after the promise of ice cream.

I might not have noticed the circular metal staircase in
the center of the room if I hadn't heard the music again:
slow, tinkling music from a partially wound music box. I
recognized the snatch of "Mary Had a Little Lamb" that
I had heard before and hurried in the direction of the
sound.

A large chimney and several stacked kitchen chairs obscured the entrance to the stairs, which led to a trap door
in the ceiling. From the dirty light filtering in through the
gable windows, I saw a small lump near the top. Even in
the darkness I could tell that it was old, a toy animal of
some kind with most of the fuzz worn away. *"...fleece was
white as snow."* The tune faded and stopped as soon as I
picked it up.

What was Will doing up here with this peculiar old toy,
and why had he dropped it on the stairs? Had he somehow managed to climb out onto the small platform on the
roof, and had the door slammed shut behind him? How
long had he been out there? My heart thundered, and I
could feel the blood pounding in my head as I pushed at
the heavy door. From the ground the cupola looked like a
fragile thing. The railings around the little platform were
old and probably rotten, and there was room for a small
child to slip between them.

"Don't move, Will!" I shouted. "I'm coming, Laura's
coming!" And the door crashed back with a bang.

It took only one glance to know that Will wasn't out
there. I poked my head above the door and looked around.
Far, far below my classmates sat in lawn chairs, stood in
clusters, and consumed tall glasses of cooling beverages;

their laughter floated up to me. I could see the church steeples of Redpath, the skeleton framework of Crybaby Bridge. The landscape shimmered in a yellow-green haze, and I dropped to my knees on the platform, dizzy with fear.

And then I noticed that one of the railings was missing. Had Will crawled out here and leaned against the decaying wooden banister?

Hugging to the floor, I inched slowly to the edge. The floor seemed to be tilting, swaying, and my stomach lurched with it. If my little cousin were in trouble in the water, I would dive in after him; if he were trapped in a burning building, nothing could hold me back. But this, this was different. Will could be sprawled unconscious on the slanted attic roof below me, and I could not make myself come within one foot of the platform's edge. I wanted to, I hated my cowardice, but I couldn't look down, couldn't raise my eyes from the floor.

"Will!" I yelled. "Will! Won't somebody help me?" But I was crying so, no one could hear me. And then the door slammed shut behind me.

ELEVEN

I THINK I SCREAMED. I worked my way back to the center of the structure and tugged frantically at the door, but it didn't open. Somehow I knew it wouldn't; someone had locked it from the inside. Why?

A board creaked under my knee, and I knelt on the floor in a praying position. The cupola was only about ten feet square, and there was nothing between me and the ground far below but a weatherbeaten floor and a narrow, crumbling railing. All I could do was wait. And yell.

It didn't take long. I heard footsteps clanging on the metal stairs, and the trap door slammed open beside me. Austin Leatherwood blinked at the sun and frowned at me. "Laura? Where in hell have you been? And why are you up here in this crazy place making such a racket? Don't you know it's dangerous up here? Nobody comes up here anymore!"

I closed my eyes against the pain of knowing. "Will? Where's Will? He ran away, came up here...."

"Will? Wiggleworm Will?" There was laughter in his voice. "Why, he's down there with everyone else, stuffing himself with food." He offered me a hand. "Well, come on, what are you waiting for? Let's go join them."

"I can't...can't stand up," I said. It hurt to breathe, and my head was whirling.

"Oh. Okay, just put your hands on my shoulders. We'll get you down." His voice, now that he understood the situation, was gentle and comforting. I did as I was told and felt myself being dragged like a sack of grain through the opening and being deposited on the hot metal step below. I gripped the railing with tight fists and, with Austin's hand on my waist, slowly descended the twisting stairs. I felt as if I were walking out of a nightmare.

"Now, see for yourself." Austin pulled back the curtain in the dim back sitting room and called my attention to the group of picnickers on the lawn. "There, isn't that Will in the yellow shorts?"

I nodded. I wanted to run out and snatch him up, never let him out of my sight. He sat at a small table with three other children while Michelle tucked a paper napkin under his chin. I smiled. Michelle should sleep well tonight.

"Well, at least I brought an extra set of clothes for Will," I said. "I never thought I'd need one for me."

Austin grinned. "You do look a mess. Why don't you do a quick clean-up, and I'll run you home for a change of clothes?" Then, after a stark appraisal of my appearance, he must have decided a quick clean-up would never do. "Or if you're not feeling up to all this partying right now, let me take you out for dinner—someplace where it's quiet. We need to talk."

I groaned. "Your wanting to talk was what got me into this mess in the first place!" I explained what had happened while I waited for him earlier.

"I'm sorry about that. Ginny waylaid me to set up tables, and it threw me behind. When I went to look for you, you weren't anywhere around."

"You didn't hear me upstairs calling Will?" I asked.

He shook his head. "No, but I heard Will screaming about having his diaper changed and the baby-sitter reading him his rights." Austin turned away from the window, smiling. "I don't thing Michelle will be having any children, at least not anytime soon."

I wondered where Will had escaped to while Michelle was chasing Gina. If that was not my little cousin I was pursuing through the attic, then who was it? Someone who wanted me out of the way for a while. Maybe permanently.

"My goodness, Laura, what in the world happened to you?" Blakely Floyd stood in the hall outside the kitchen with a chocolate cake in her hands. Her lips were pink and glossy, her dress immaculate, and she smelled like bath powder. Not a smudge of dirt anywhere, not even a granule. I knew where I'd like to see that cake, and it wasn't in her hands.

She smiled. "Ginny finally gave up on you, so I pitched in to help with the food," she told me.

"How sweet of you," I said. I had forgotten all about Ginny. Well, I would explain later; she would understand.

"What happened?" Blakely repeated. "You look like you've been crawling in the cellar."

"Think higher," I said, and marched into the bathroom. I winced at what I saw: spider webs in my hair, dirt on my face, grime under my fingernails, and a splinter in my knee. Not even the strongest bleach could save my once-white shorts.

By the time I cleaned off the top layer of dirt, Michelle was bringing her charges back to the house to scrape off the remains of their supper.

"My gosh, what happened to you?" she squealed. I was really getting tired of that question.

"You asked me to go upstairs to look for Will, remember? It hasn't been cleaned up there since Hoover was President."

She looked blank. She probably thought Hoover invented the vacuum cleaner. "By the way, where did you find him?" I asked.

Michelle giggled. "In that closet under the stairs; you should've seen him! He had put on this huge pair of old rubber boots, and he was hiding in there wearing them and nothing else, just as naked as—"

"I wish you had told me," I said. "I was worried to death."

She shrugged. "Sorry, I just forgot."

"Did you happen to see anyone else go upstairs?" I asked. "I could have sworn I heard somebody up there." I helped her lead the children into the bathroom and held them up to the sink one at a time.

Michelle swiped at a chocolaty face with a damp cloth. "Well, Mr. Leatherwood went up there—you know, young Mr. Leatherwood—but he came right down; and that strange one, Miss Delia, she wandered around like she was looking for somebody." Michelle frowned. "She gives me the creeps! In fact, this whole place gives me the creeps."

I had to agree with her there.

"And Blakely Floyd and that other lady, Ginny whatever-her-name-is," she continued. "They were in and out with a bunch of other people. I guess any of them could've gone up there. Why?"

I dried Will's face and hands and scrambled in my handbag for a five-dollar bill. The girl deserved a bonus. "Just curious," I said, "and thanks."

Aunt Nell was in the backyard weeding her flowers when we got home. "You're back earlier than I expected," she said, stooping to give Will a kiss.

I stayed well behind the screen door so she couldn't see my disheveled appearance. "I'm going to take a quick shower," I told her. "Austin and I are going out for a bite to eat. We need to talk." I didn't add "about Laney," but I might as well have. My aunt nodded. She understood.

The hot shower was wonderful, and the cold drink that followed was even better. I barely had time to blow dry my hair and pull a cool cotton dress over my head before Austin came by for me. We drove to a small restaurant that specialized in Italian food in a town about thirty miles away and sipped our drinks in a booth by the window with a candle flickering between us. I felt a little awkward being in such a romantic setting with Austin Leatherwood. My cousin had died over three months ago, but Austin was still her property. As far as I was concerned he might as well have a big *L* stenciled on his forehead.

I had often gone out with my cousin and her then-steady boyfriend on double dates, or even as a threesome, but it had been years since the two of us had gone anywhere alone. I smiled, wondering if Austin remembered our one and only date in the ninth grade. He had invited me on a hayride sponsored by his Boy Scout troop, and I had been miserable the whole time, first afraid that he might try to kiss me and then disappointed that he didn't.

"What's so funny?"

Austin's words startled me, and I took a swallow of my drink before answering. "I was just thinking of something that happened a long time ago," I said.

"I'm glad you can find something to smile about after your little adventure this afternoon," he said. "Do you feel like talking about it now?"

I felt queasy just thinking about it; it would be easy to make a joke about what had happened, to pass it off as an accident, but it wasn't an accident. Someone had lured me to the rooftop on purpose and locked the door behind me, someone who knew about my fear of heights. And that someone could be Austin Leatherwood.

I decided to face the issue head on. "You'll probably think I'm crazy," I began, "but somebody locked me out on that cupola today. I couldn't open the door, Austin."

"Laura, that door wasn't locked. Look, you were hot and tired and frightened, and that thing must weigh a ton—"

"Then who shut it?" I snapped. "Who led me up there making me think I was following Will? Who wound that music box and left it on the stairs? Music boxes don't wind themselves!" I resented his condescending attitude, and I disliked being used in someone's horrible idea of a game.

Austin didn't answer because the waitress came and took our orders, then returned with a carafe of red wine. As I sipped it, my tension eased, and Austin seemed more responsive.

"You said something about a music box," he reminded me. "What music box?"

Until now I'd forgotten it. "It was near the top of those spiral stairs," I said, "and someone had wound it just enough to play part of a tune. Didn't you see it? I dropped it right where I found it."

He shook his head. "No, but it could have fallen to the floor below. I can check later, if you like."

He was humoring me again; well, let him! "It was a stuffed animal," I told him, "an old one, and it played 'Mary Had a Little Lamb.' I didn't see it when we left the attic because, to tell you the truth, I didn't look; I was in too big a hurry to get out of that place."

"If it's still there, I'll find it." Austin started to touch my arm, then changed his mind. "Don't worry, Laura. We'll find out what's going on."

"It won't be there," I said. "It was probably gone before you ever got there this afternoon. Whoever left that music box on the stairs wanted me to see it and no one else. I think that toy has served its purpose."

Austin started to saw off a slice of bread and stopped with the knife in the crust. "Laney heard music, too," he said. "She said it had a kind of faraway, tinny sound."

"Like a child's music box," I answered.

In spite of my squeamish stomach from the afternoon, I managed to put away a small spinach salad and a large plate of veal scallopini while Austin did justice to his broiled flounder. Both of us seemed to be postponing the inevitable question of Laney's death.

After the meal Austin folded his arms and leaned against his corner of the booth. "I just want to know two things," he said. "If someone really did lure you to the cupola today, how did they know you were going to be in the house at that particular time?" His eyes never left mine. "And how could they possibly have known Will was going to run off and hide?"

"Maybe they heard you ask me to meet you there," I said. "I mentioned it to several people myself; it was no secret." I took a sip of coffee and glanced at the reflection of the candle in the dark window. Night had finally come.

"As for Will's running away," I continued, "I think it just happened at an opportune time, and whoever was up there took advantage of it." I leaned forward, challenging his bold stare. "He, or she, was up there, Austin, poking around upstairs when I came inside looking for you. I don't know what they wanted or why they were there, but they knew I would follow the sound of that music box, and they were right."

Austin looked away. "Do you think it was someone at Willowbend? One of the family?"

"Not necessarily. It could have been anybody." I told him of my visit with Junior Pittman and about what I had done to Buddy Callahan, and he laughed.

"Buddy knows I'm terrified of heights," I reminded him. "Remember that time we all went out to Crybaby Bridge?"

His face went white. I had finally mentioned the subject we had come here to discuss, yet neither of us knew how to begin.

"Why did she do it?" he whispered. "I still...I just can't believe Laney would do such a thing! Laura, do you think she killed herself?"

"I don't know." Tears blurred my vision, and I fumbled for a tissue. Did I really want to know? "She told me Amanda wanted to meet her there, that she had received a note from her."

He frowned. "What happened to the note? Did anyone ever see it?"

"No one; maybe it went in the water with her, but there *was* an Amanda, Austin, and there was a locket. That much is true."

Austin nodded. "I know. She showed me the locket, told me about the little girl Amanda. Mother said she used to live in the old tenant cabin." He smoothed the crumpled napkin and refolded it, pressing the creases through his fingers. "But Amanda is dead, Laura. She died years ago."

"In the Enoree, like Laney," I said, "and everyone seems to have conveniently forgotten how."

"My God, Laura!" Austin set his cup down with a clatter. "You don't think Laney's death had anything to do with Amanda, do you?"

Maybe it was the wine, but my head was aching and heavy. I wanted to put my face down on the starched white tablecloth and go to sleep. "We have three choices," I said. "Laney fabricated the story about Amanda and got carried away with her own myth—"

"You mean she was chasing a phantom when she fell, or jumped, from the bridge?" Austin rubbed his eyes. He looked almost as tired as I felt. "That's hard to believe," he said, "even for Laney."

"I didn't say I believed it," I said. "That's just one way it could have happened, and although none of us likes to suggest it, there's also the possibility of suicide." I made myself say the word; it came out in a hoarse whisper.

"But why?" He faced me squarely across the candle's wavering flame.

"I don't know why," I said, "and I was probably closer to Laney than anyone. Things went on in that mind of hers that we'll never understand."

Austin stared silently out the window as the waitress refilled our coffee cups. "She got pretty depressed at times," he said, "but she always bounded back."

"You were with her more than I was those last few months," I said. "Was anything worrying her more than usual? Could you tell any difference in the way she acted?"

"Well, she was all wrapped up in that Amanda thing, and she seemed to be excited about her practice with Doc Ratteree. No, I don't think she was depressed, but they found liquor in her house, remember? And Laney never used to drink. Alcohol can have a strange effect on people, especially if they're not used to it." He glanced up sharply. "You said she told you about a note; when was that?"

"The night before she died. She phoned me in Atlanta, said she'd found a note from Amanda in the cabin." I shivered in spite of the hot coffee. "I thought she was teasing at first, or that someone was playing a joke on her. I never thought she'd actually take it seriously.''

He frowned. ''I wonder why she didn't mention it to me. Did she tell you what it said?''

''Something like, 'If you want to help, be at Crybaby Bridge tomorrow night,' and it gave a time—ten o'clock, I think—and it was signed Amanda.'' I drew my sweater around me. ''Amanda died at Crybaby Bridge, too.''

''So there is a connection.'' His sigh was so despairing, I wanted to comfort him, but I didn't know how.

I followed him mutely to the car, waiting for him to speak, but he didn't say anything more until we stopped for traffic before leaving the parking lot. ''Tell me everything you know about Amanda,'' he said, and I did.

Austin drove silently for a while. ''It's peculiar,'' he said. ''Except for Miss Annie, all the people you've talked with about Amanda are from my own family, yet until recently I'd never heard of her.''

''Why should you have? She wasn't a relative.''

''Have you talked with my grandfather about this?'' he asked.

''No, I was hoping to see him today, but I decided to spend my time on the roof instead,'' I said.

''You didn't think that was so funny this afternoon.'' He dimmed his lights at the oncoming traffic. ''The old man's been around a long time. If anyone remembers what happened to Amanda, he should—if he'll only cooperate.''

''I want to go with you when you talk with him,'' I said, and he agreed. I didn't want to admit it to Austin, but I preferred my information firsthand where Laney was concerned. ''And I plan to talk with Doc Ratteree, too,'' I added. ''Laney might have said something to him, and we need all the facts we can scrape together. Besides, Ve-

suvius is about to run out of heartworm pills. It will give
me an excuse to drop by."

"With this reunion dance tomorrow night, I won't have
much time until Sunday," he said. "But if you aren't doing
anything we can drive out to Willowbend after lunch, as
long as we give His Grace plenty of time for his afternoon
snooze."

I laughed. I hadn't heard Austin refer to his grandfather that way in years, and for just a brief, bittersweet
moment I pretended we were all back in high school and
Laney was with us again.

"By the way," Austin said as we wound through the
quiet streets of Redpath, "when we were in the restaurant, you mentioned a third possibility for Laney's death,
but you never said what it was."

"Probably because I don't even like to think of it, much
less speak of it," I said. "But there's also a chance that
someone forced Laney off Crybaby Bridge, that someone
might have pushed her into the river that night."

"But why?"

"That's what I came home to find out," I admitted.

TWELVE

THE VETERINARIAN'S waiting room wasn't crowded, but I had to wait until Doc Ratteree could see me. I paid for the pills for Vesuvius and took a chair between a buxom woman cooing to a trembling poodle and a small boy with a sleeping kitten on his lap.

Soon a huge boxer dragged his owner from one of the examining rooms and zipped through the door to the parking lot and freedom. A few minutes later, Doc Ratteree poked his head around the door of the cubicle and called my name.

"I thought we could talk while I worked," he said, offering me the one chair. He was a large, ruddy-faced man with sloping shoulders and a gruff voice, but his big hands were surprisingly gentle as they covered mine.

"I can't even begin to tell you how much I miss your cousin," he said. "She was a bright spot in my life."

I watched as he swept bits of gauze and litter from the floor and disinfected the metal table. He glanced at me over his shoulder. "I haven't seen your aunt since the funeral, but I hear she's holding up well. How have you been, Laura? Is there something I can do to help?"

"I hope so," I said, and told him about Amanda. "Did Laney ever mention her to you?"

He tossed a crumpled paper towel into the trash can. "No, I don't believe she did."

"She was a little girl who lived here about forty years ago," I explained. "Laney found her locket."

"Locket! Yes, of course she did! She showed it to me one day, showed me the inscription inside, but I'd forgotten the child's name. To tell you the truth, things are so hectic around here that Laney and I rarely had time to discuss anything except the business at hand."

Doc Ratteree briskly washed his hands. "I didn't know the child, as I wasn't raised here." He smiled. "It only seems like I've been here forever."

He turned and leaned against the sink. "Laney was determined to find out all about her. I wonder if she ever did." His eyes grew moist as he spoke, and he made a great noise throwing instruments into a pan. "God, I miss her, and not just because of the workload. I just miss *her*, Laney, miss her spirit."

I nodded. "So do I."

"While you're here, let me introduce you to Dr. Marshall, who's helping me this summer." He motioned for me to follow him to the adjoining room, where I heard a low, soothing voice and the whimper of a frightened animal.

A tall, bearded young man was examining a squirming cocker spaniel while the patient's owner looked on anxiously. He turned and smiled at me when his name was mentioned, but he was too occupied to do more than speak.

"Sidney Marshall, Laura Graham. Laura is Laney McCall's cousin," he explained. "She has an interesting black Lab named Vesuvius that we might be seeing sometime this summer," he added, smiling. "You're going to stay with us for a while, aren't you, Laura?"

"Probably," I said, "at least until I can get my car repaired." I spoke briefly to the young veterinarian, as I could see he didn't have time just then for idle chatter.

"He just got back from two years in the Peace Corps," the older doctor explained as he walked with me to my car. "He's agreed to help me out temporarily, but I wish I could convince him to stay." He winked at me. "He's single, you know, and not bad looking. I don't suppose you'd be interested in a summer romance?"

I laughed. "Give me a break, Doc! You'll have to use some other bait." The young vet was attractive, but there was something about him that bothered me, something I couldn't put my finger on.

But I didn't have time to wonder about him long because I had given Ginny Adair my absolute word of honor that I'd compensate for my slackness the day before and help the banquet committee decorate for the reunion dance. I didn't tell her exactly what had happened at the picnic except to say that Will had led me on a "wild-goose chase."

The party was to be at Charley's Place, a rustic spot set back in the pine woods where large groups of Redpath's citizens had celebrated for as long as I could remember.

The long, paneled room was decorated with streamers and balloons in our class colors of gold and white, and mementos from our high school days were displayed on a table at one end of the room. Snapshots contributed by classmates covered a bulletin board under large construction paper letters that read: THE WAY WE WERE.

Laney's face leaped out at me: in a pyramid pose with other cheerleaders with a goal post in the background; dancing in a slinky red dress with Austin at the prom; swinging like a chimpanzee from the wild cherry tree in the schoolyard with a banana in her hand. I closed my eyes and swallowed. The party was going to be dull without her.

Another classmate and I placed daisies in a white bud vase tied with a gold ribbon at each table, and I set up a welcome station for the name tags near the door. Austin had reluctantly agreed to use them after I convinced him that not only would they benefit our dates and spouses, but would also save me from having to explain a lie to Junior Pittman.

I rushed home from decorating, fed Vesuvius, showered, and changed into the bold turquoise cocktail dress I had bought for the occasion, then drove back to Charley's Place in record time. I was there to greet the first guests with those obnoxious sticky-back labels that few people bothered to wear.

They drifted in by twos and threes: tall and short, black and white, fat and thin, intelligent and not so intelligent. All seemed happy to be together again, and the majority of them had changed only slightly in appearance over the last ten years. We had such a small class, I knew all my classmates by name and could have arranged most of them in their usual seats if called upon to do so.

I had gone through twelve years of school with some of these people, and they were an important part of my life. I thought I knew them well. But did I? Could one of this laughing, chattering group be the person who tricked me onto the rotting cupola at Willowbend? Had it been a classmate who followed me from Ginny's that night?

Blakely Floyd in a trim yellow linen that showed off her tan sipped a diet drink (I heard her order it) and listened to one classmate's anecdotes while she followed another with her eyes. The other was Austin, who was exchanging hunting stories with a group of fellow good old boys and was apparently unaware that he was being watched. Austin owned an ancient rattletrap of a pickup truck and two beautiful Brittany spaniels named Jeb and Sal, who accompanied him on weekend hunting trips, and he was one of the few men I knew who could discuss hunting and literature with equal enthusiasm.

My drink needed refilling, but I hated to leave my post at the door, and since the only person handy was Buddy Callahan, I avoided his attention. When Junior Pittman wandered by, I held out my glass. "I sure would like another drink," I said, "but I'd die before I'd ask for it."

He stood there for a minute, trying to decide if I had cracked a joke. Finally he smiled. "I haven't forgotten about that dance later, Laura. Can I get you some punch?"

"Gin and tonic, please," I said, "with a slice of lime."

Junior frowned. "You didn't drink in high school."

"My parents wouldn't let me," I said, "but I'm old enough now."

He brought me the drink and set it in front of me with his mouth in a disapproving line. I didn't think I would have to worry about dancing with Junior that night.

He was a grim sort who took everything seriously. I wondered if he disliked Laney enough to take revenge on me. I had turned down his offer of a date, and he knew when and where I was meeting Austin and had had plenty of opportunity to get upstairs before me.

For that matter, so did Blakely Floyd, and she was spiteful enough to have done it, too. But how had she managed to stay so clean? I smiled, thinking of Blakely creeping around the attic, sweltering in a protective smock and gloves.

From the other side of the room Buddy Callahan guffawed loudly and slapped his beefy leg. Wanda Simpson, who had lost thirty pounds and had her hair styled for the reunion, giggled and clung to his arm. Later I saw them dancing together, and much later he even smiled and waved at me. I smiled back, forgiven.

But had he forgiven me yesterday afternoon when the beer steamed from his pants and classmates laughed behind his back?

Austin had saved me a place at his table with the Adairs and another couple. Blakely cast little sidelong glances from across the room while we ate. As much as I disliked the woman, I would gladly have changed places with her that night.

Before we served ourselves in the buffet line, our class president called for a moment of silence in Laney's memory, and for the rest of the evening she might as well have been sitting at our table.

It wasn't much fun partying with a ghost.

THIRTEEN

I WAS NOT LOOKING FORWARD to spending another afternoon at Willowbend, and at the risk of hurting his feelings, I said as much to Austin as we drove there that Sunday.

He laughed. "It is kind of spooky looking, but it's really a right comfortable old house. Don't worry—I won't let the phantom of the attic get you this time."

"Huh!" I said. For all I knew he or one of his weird relatives could be the so-called "phantom of the attic." The Squires were a peculiar assortment, and according to Aunt Nell, all were dominated by their father, the judge.

"Does your grandfather know we're coming?" I asked, hoping in a way that he wouldn't be expecting us, that none of them would be at home.

Austin smiled at me as we turned into the long, narrow drive at Willowbend. "He knows we're coming," he said, "but he doesn't know why. It's best to catch the old boy off guard."

The ugly mustard-colored house squatted at the end of the drive with the tall hedge like a prickly collar around it. It was not quite as hot as it had been the day of the picnic because of a slight breeze and overcast skies, but the humidity was high, and my dress stuck to me in spite of the air-conditioned car.

The family waited for us in the large front parlor, which Austin pointed out was rarely used except for Sundays and holidays. Judge Decatur Squires sat in an ancient Morris chair that must have been the original version of a recliner and that was probably the only comfortable seat in the room. He frowned as he read the Columbia paper, apparently not liking what he saw, and tossed it impatiently aside when we entered.

"Laura, isn't it?" He rose quickly and crossed the room to greet me; a slender man of medium height, he seemed unusually fit for someone in his late seventies.

I had seen him often in Redpath since he still kept an office in town, and I had met him on several social occasions, but it had been several years since I had talked with him, and I was surprised at how little he had changed. Although his hair was white and thinning, I could remember when it had been even redder than Austin's. His eyes, behind bifocals, were a keen, snapping blue.

Miss Delia, in a cloud of pink georgette, served a refreshing mint-tasting punch with Scotch shortbread cut in squares, still warm from the oven. I suspected she had baked it just because we were coming.

Mr. Nevin Squires crept in, a slight gray ghost in a striped seersucker with a white rosebud in his lapel. He smelled of Old Spice aftershave and sat gingerly in a small rosewood side chair that would have been too fragile for a larger man.

I felt a little like Alice at the Queen's birthday party, as Austin and I were the only ones in casual dress, but since it didn't seem to bother Austin, I decided it wasn't important.

The five of us chatted pleasantly about the class reunion, the weather, and my Aunt Nell's health while Austin and I competed in a duel of hesitation, each waiting for the other to bring up the subject of Amanda.

I finally gave up and took the plunge. "Judge Squires," I began, "do you remember a little girl named Amanda who used to live in the old cabin?"

The old man went rigid. He set his punch glass on the small marble-topped table at his side and sat straight up in his chair. "Why do you want to know about Amanda?" His voice was harsh, but his eyes were sad. "The child is dead; leave her be."

The silence was so heavy in the room, I felt as if the ceiling were pressing on my head. Miss Delia took the opportunity to make a quick getaway. "Let me cut some roses for you," she said to me in a too-bright voice. "You can take some to your aunt."

I wanted to follow her out of the room. I wanted to walk with her in the sweet, sunlit garden. I wanted to escape. Instead, I turned back to the judge.

"I'm sorry if I upset you, Judge Squires, but this child was important to my cousin, and she's important to me. I have to find out how she died. It might have something to do with Laney's death."

"I don't see how. That child died years before your cousin was even born. She drowned right out there in the Enoree." The judge leaned back and closed his eyes. I got the impression that he thought we all were going to hell in a handbasket and that I was first in line.

Austin squirmed in his chair, which, like mine, was an uncomfortable Victorian upholstered in maroon velvet. "Grandfather, do you remember how it happened?" he asked.

"I just said she drowned. That's all I know." The judge looked briefly at his grandson; his eyes dared him to go further. "She fell from Crybaby Bridge," he said in a barely audible voice.

I felt a sick, plunging sensation in my stomach. The room was muggy and close, and dust motes swam in the narrow slant of sunlight that squeezed between heavy draperies. I was a prisoner of the hard, scratchy chair, the dark, oppressive room. If I didn't get out soon, I was going to suffocate.

Austin must have understood my silent appeal because he came and stood beside me. "Are you familiar with anyone named Lee?" he asked the judge. "Someone whose last name begins with the letter *C*? It was on the child's locket."

"Her locket?" I could tell from his expression that this was the first he'd heard of the locket, unless he was a very good actor.

"Laney found it in the old cabin where Amanda used to live," I said. "The name Lee and the initial *C* were engraved on the inside."

He looked at me silently for a long time. "How on earth could it matter now?" he asked.

"I don't know," I said, "but it does."

He turned away from me toward the window, from which it was impossible to see anything except a narrow strip of the enclosing hedge. "I don't know anyone named Lee," he said, and I knew we would learn no more from him that day.

"What now?" Austin whispered as we waited in the kitchen for his Aunt Delia to find a jar for her roses.

"I think I'll check Laney's place again. I could've missed something before, and the painters will be coming soon." I groaned. It seemed that every place I had been lately was unbearably hot and stuffy. "I might as well go tonight and get it over with. I'll pack some of her things while I'm there."

"You're not going alone? I don't think that's such a good idea," he said. "Why don't—"

"Now, watch those thorns," Aunt Delia said. "Do you think you can get this home without spilling it? Austin, you will be careful how you drive?"

"Yes, ma'am, I promise." He kissed her cheek and slipped out the kitchen door. "I've got to run upstairs a minute. Be right back." He meant for his aunt to think he was going to the bathroom, but I knew he was going to the attic to see if the music box was still there.

Miss Delia and I stood in the kitchen, the silence awkward between us. She seemed to want to tell me something but didn't know how to begin.

"What is it, Miss Delia?" I whispered.

Her eyes darted past me as if she were afraid we'd be overheard. The woman was frightened in her own house! Slowly she hung her smock on the pantry door and tossed bits of rose stems into the trash. "That music you mentioned..."

"The music Laney heard?"

She nodded. "It was Amanda's, Amanda's music—"

"Did it sound like a music box?" I asked eagerly. "Miss Delia, please—"

"Be sure and have Austin let us know the next time you're coming, and we'll make ice cream," Miss Delia said. "And maybe your aunt will come, too." She was looking past me again.

Her brother stood behind me. "I hope you'll make it soon," he said. "I'll even turn the freezer. Delia makes wonderful ice cream."

I smiled. "I'll keep that in mind." Across the hall in the sitting room I heard the judge moving about, and then the sound of a television baseball game. Who was this woman afraid of?

Austin stood at the foot of the stairs, and his face told me he had found nothing in the attic. I wasn't surprised.

"What's the matter with your Aunt Delia?" I asked after we had said our good-byes and started back to Redpath. "She acts like she's scared of her shadow."

"She's intimidated," he said. "My grandfather intimidates everyone, including me. Even my mother is a little afraid of him."

"Why?"

He shrugged. "It's the way they were brought up. Aunt Delia and Uncle Nevin have spent their lives trying to please him; Mother, too, to a certain extent, but she married and got out of the house.

"The peculiar thing is, the more they try to please him, the less he appreciates them." He slammed his hand against the steering wheel. "It infuriates me sometimes! Aunt Delia wasn't always like that, you know. Mother said she had a fine old time in college, but she made the mistake of letting Grandfather find out about it, and home she went!"

"He took her out of school for having fun?" I asked.

Austin smiled. "Found out she'd been going to river parties and drinking Purple Passion," he said. "He soon put an end to that.

"And you know what a likable person Uncle Nevin is," he added. "Shy and intellectual, and he doesn't make much money, but he's happy with his work."

I agreed. "I can't imagine him anywhere else but in the library."

"His father wanted him to play football in high school; can you imagine? He wanted him to go to law school. And he tried both, but they didn't work out."

"And your Aunt Delia?" I asked. "What did he want her to be?"

"Just what she is," he said. "a household drudge."

"Your grandfather knows something about Amanda. Couldn't you tell? I wonder if he knows what caused her to fall? From the way he reacted, she must have been more than a tenant's child."

He glanced at me. "Maybe she was his. She would be about the right age."

"But who was the mother? Surely not slovenly Mrs. Scoggins!"

"I don't know, but her birth should be on record at the courthouse," he suggested. "That is, if she was born in this county." Austin slowed as he turned into my aunt's street. "And surely there was something in the paper about her death."

"You're right," I said. "I'll check those out tomorrow, but first I'll see what I can find out at Laney's."

Austin opened the car door for me. "Do you think you should go alone?" he asked. "I'm not crazy about the idea of going out there again, but I will if you feel uneasy about going by yourself."

"Don't worry, I don't plan to be there long," I assured him. For some reason, I felt as if this were something I had to do alone. I didn't mention it to Austin, but there was something beguiling about the place; not the cottage, but the vine-entangled cabin behind it. The mystery of it gripped me, as it had my cousin, and I knew I had to go there by myself.

FOURTEEN

AUNT NELL lifted the last piece of crisp bacon from the frying pan and poured the grease into a can. "You're not telling me everything," she announced.

"About what?" I was peeling a tomato for sandwiches, red ripe and just picked from the plant by the back fence.

"About Laney's death, about Amanda." She spoke softly as Will was playing in the next room.

I was tempted to go on lying, but she had a right to know. "Amanda died in the Enoree, like Laney," I said. "She must have been a special child, different; even the judge remembers her. I don't know what her relationship with the Squires family is, but I intend to find out."

"Do you think this has anything to do with the way your cousin died?" She stacked toast on a plate, one piece at a time.

"Laney was asking questions. She had talked with Miss Annie, and with Delia Squires; Daisy Leatherwood, too."

She poured iced tea into tall glasses. "What about the judge?"

"No," I said. "I don't think she'd gotten that far yet. If she had, she didn't tell him about the locket."

My aunt stood close behind me; her hand was cool on my wrist. "Laura, do you think Laney discovered something she wasn't supposed to know?"

"I'm not sure," I said. "That's what I'm trying to find out."

"Well, I don't like it," my aunt said, "not one little bit! Let's just forget about it, Laura; it's not worth it. We'll tell the police what we know and let them handle it." She leaned against the counter, pulling a red-striped dish towel through her hands. "The last thing I want is to put you in danger. You can't handle this alone."

I kissed her cheek. "Tell the police what?" I asked. "We don't know anything to tell them. Besides, I'm not alone. Austin's helping."

She backed away from me. "But he's the link! Don't you see that, Laura? Austin Leatherwood is the link between something that happened long ago in his family and Laney's death."

I thought about what she had said as I drove to Laney's that evening. I couldn't believe Austin Leatherwood would ever hurt Laney, or anyone else for that matter. And he seemed as interested in finding out how Laney died as my aunt was. He was certainly doing all he could to help me solve the puzzle of Amanda. I had pointed this out to Aunt Nell, but I don't think I convinced her.

I did convince her that Laney's belongings needed to be packed and given away before the painters came. The Rileys had been lenient about allowing her things to remain where they were, but I knew their patience would eventually run out.

"It has to be done," I told my aunt, "and I might as well go on and get started tonight. It's too hot out there in the daytime." And so I went, against her protests, but I had to promise to take Vesuvius with me. He sat behind me as I drove with his paws on the back of my seat and his cold black nose nudging my neck.

"You silly thing!" I said, reaching up to rub his head. "You're a bigger coward than I am, but what Aunt Nell doesn't know won't hurt her."

For all my talk of braveness, I felt a little apprehensive as I pulled into Laney's dusky carport. The house, though sweltering and dusty, had not been disturbed since my last visit. Whoever had been there before had either found what they were looking for or had decided it wasn't there.

While Vesuvius slept across the front step, I lugged in empty grocery boxes to hold Laney's belongings. It was still light outside at eight o'clock, but I switched on every light in the house, thinking maybe it wouldn't have been such a bad idea to ask Austin or Ginny Adair along to help.

The bathroom was the easiest room to tackle, so I started in there. Laney used hardly any makeup and was seldom sick, so there was very little in the way of cosmetics and medicine to pack. I recognized a tube of my own toothpaste, rolled in my special way, and tossed it into a box with things to throw away, along with most of Laney's towels, which were a flimsy lot left over from college.

My aunt could probably use the few cans of food left in the kitchen, and the two of us could decide later what to do with Laney's cooking utensils. My cousin cooked only when inspired, and since her periods of inspiration came at infrequent intervals, many of her gadgets were shiny new, and some probably hadn't been used at all.

After Laney discovered quiche, she had served it at every gathering for months, and I knew for a fact that she had once lived for a week off a batch of lasagna. I found myself smiling, relating certain foods to periods in our lives, and when the tears came, I wiped them away with party napkins that said HAVE YOU HUGGED YOUR VET TODAY?

But when I opened the cabinet over the stove and recognized my mother's chipped set of dishes, I quickly shut the cabinet doors and walked away. The dishes, which had a pattern of brightly colored fruits, were always a favorite of Laney's, and Mother had given them to her when they moved.

I wandered to the living room and stood in the doorway watching twilight deepen as all around me frogs and cicadas filled the night with their sleepy noises. When Vesuvius decided he wanted to come in, I was glad to have his company. I liked the comfortable sound of his feet padding behind me as I walked through the silent house.

We had already taken Will's things to Aunt Nell's, so I turned to my cousin's room but could get no farther than the doorway. It was almost as if Laney were sitting there cross-legged on the bold, blue-striped bedspread, laughing over the antics of some animal she had tended during the day. Laney liked animals because they amused her, just as people did, only animals didn't care.

I forced myself to open the rolltop desk that my aunt and uncle had given her in high school and gathered the handful of letters and her address book to pack away, discarding a drawer full of old rubber bands, bent paper clips, and dried-up ballpoint pens. A copy of the alumni news from our college was jammed in the back of a bottom drawer. When I pulled it out, I discovered a card wedged inside. It was a notice from the county library, the usual "Have you forgotten?" kind sent out when a book is overdue. Underneath the familiar printed reminder was a handwritten message:

WILL BE GLAD TO PICK THIS UP ON MY
WAY IN TO WORK THIS WEEK

And it was signed Nevin Squires. I looked at the postmark dated the week before Laney died, and a terrible, lonely sadness washed over me. Why had Nevin Squires told me he hadn't talked with my cousin? Had he forgotten about the card, or had his stay in the hospital been an emergency that he hadn't planned on when he wrote the message?

I tucked the card into my pocketbook. I only wanted to finish here and go home.

I moved sluggishly to Laney's closet and slid back the door. The faint odor of cigarette smoke still hung there, mixed with the cool green scent of her perfume. I touched a long, bulky jacket knitted of purple wool; it was worn but expensive and a favorite of Laney's. I couldn't imagine anyone else wearing it.

I softly closed the closet door. If I gave away Laney's things, that meant she would never come back. The purple jacket was my cousin's. She had worn it to ball games and movies and to classes in college. She had taken long walks in it on winter evenings and had thrown it over her shoulders on chilly mornings. She loved it, and it was hers, but she would never wear it again because she was dead.

"Laney is dead." I said it aloud, and felt as if someone had slapped me with a cold hand. I would come back for the boxes later. I had to get out of this house! My hand was on the light switch when I heard the sound—the music box sound—and it was coming from outside the house.

FIFTEEN

AMANDA, OR SOMEONE who wanted me to think she was Amanda, waited in the murky light at the far end of the yard. I turned off the bedroom lamp and stood at the window listening to the toy's tinkling song.

Mary had a little lamb, little lamb. . . .

Vesuvius growled low in his throat, and I was glad Aunt Nell had made me bring him. Someone—it looked like a small girl in a white dress—stood in the shadow of a mimosa tree that grew at the edge of the old cabin road. It was still not quite dark outside, but I could just distinguish the stuffed animal in her arms. As the tune slowly wound to a stop, she turned and walked up the hill, then paused. She seemed to be looking back, waiting for me to follow.

I swallowed the knot in my throat and felt it all the way to my stomach. The last time I had followed the music box tune, I had ended up on top of the roof at Willowbend. But if I didn't find out what she wanted, I might never have another opportunity. Besides, I had Vesuvius with me now, and I wasn't about to be led onto any high places.

I remembered seeing a flashlight in the kitchen and ran to get it, hoping the batteries were still good. They were, and I stood in the hallway wondering what to do about Vesuvius. If I let him run free, he might frighten away my "ghost," but I hadn't thought to bring a leash.

By now the dog had sensed my agitation and had begun to bark and dash back and forth to the front screen door. Quickly I grabbed one of my cousin's leather belts and at-

tached it to his collar. It was all I could do to hold him
back as we raced around the house and up the crude dirt
road.

The paleness of the child's gown stood out against the
dark walls as we circled past the crumbling cabin. I was
glad we wouldn't be stopping there, as I could imagine the
rats that had taken up residence under the floor. I shuddered as foliage brushed my face and branches clawed at
my bare legs. I didn't like being touched by things I
couldn't see.

Where was I being led? And why? Amanda (I thought
of her as Amanda because I didn't know what else to call
her) seemed to know where she was going and marched
resolutely ahead, a silent little specter, allowing me to get
no closer than following distance. Once when she ducked
out of sight behind some trees, I thought I had lost her,
until I heard once again the haunting nursery song. Had
she led my cousin on the same twilight quest?

We crossed a footbridge over a narrow stream trickling
its way to the Enoree. Vesuvius romped at my side, enjoying his curious evening stroll; he seemed to have abandoned the reason for our adventure for all the wonderful
little scents and noises he discovered along the way.

We walked past a field of waist-high corn, its green
leaves whispering, and skirted a barbed-wire fence enclosing the Squireses' far pasture. The small white figure
dipped behind a low hill, and I followed slowly, my hand
on the dog's collar to keep him from lunging ahead.

Cedars ringed the wrought-iron fence surrounding the
family graveyard. A tall marble stone stood in the center
as if commanding respect from the smaller, more modest
markers. I caught a flash of white moving in and out
among the graves and the giant oaks that guarded them.
The rusty gate hung open, and I stood there casting my

frail light about while listening for the muted chime of the music box song.

But it wasn't the music box I heard; it was the low, rushing sound of the Enoree just beyond where the land leveled off into boggy pine ground. And beyond that, beyond the mounds of trees hovering over the water, reared the forbidding skeletal framework of Crybaby Bridge.

If Vesuvius's barking hadn't jarred me out of the helpless, desolate feeling that took hold of me, I don't know how long I would have stood there, but I looked up to see Amanda waiting in a deep shadow a few yards away with her small hand on a gravestone, and something inside me crumbled. I didn't care who she was or what might happen; I only knew I had to try to put things right.

Again the dog growled, but his barking turned to a whine as I softly spoke to him and shone my light on the stone. The inscription on the moss-covered granite read:

ADA MARY SQUIRES
B. APRIL 11, 1917 D. SEPT. 3, 1942
TO ERR IS HUMAN, TO FORGIVE DIVINE.

"What?" I spoke aloud. "This isn't Amanda's grave!" I had been looking for a child's grave, but a woman was buried here. What did she have to do with Amanda? And then I remembered Miss Annie's words. Ada Squires was the judge's pretty younger sister who had died of rheumatic fever. She would have been just the right age to be Amanda's mother.

I stood, feeling very much alone in the now-dark cemetery. "Is this what you wanted me to see?" I asked, but no one answered because no one was there. Amanda had disappeared, but she had left her toy behind. I found the threadbare lamb playing its lonely song in a far corner of the graveyard on a small grave set apart from the rest. Someone, probably Delia Squires, had planted a fragrant rosebush at its foot, and at the head, beneath a pathetic stone lamb, was the name Mary Amanda and nothing else.

SIXTEEN

IT TOOK ALMOST AN HOUR to get back to Laney's following the backroads, but at least I could see where I was going. The dim yellow lights of Willowbend winked at me through the dark hedge as I went by, and if it hadn't been so late and if I hadn't been so tired, I would have pounded on the door and demanded to know about Ada Squires and why Amanda had been buried apart from the rest.

Not a car passed me until I reached the main road, and by then I could see the lights from Laney's house. For once I was sorry my cousin had been a teetotaler. I could have used a good, stiff drink.

I settled instead for a strong cup of tea and a hot shower at Aunt Nell's, where I used about half a bottle of calamine lotion on the chigger bites on my legs and ankles. I put the musical lamb and the library notice in the back of my dresser drawer with Amanda's locket and climbed into bed, expecting to lie awake haunted by child ghosts and dark, misty water. I slept.

"Vesuvius and I went for a little walk last night," I explained to my aunt the next morning. How did one account for seeing a ghost? In the first place, I didn't even believe in ghosts, and the bright morning sunshine mocked what had seemed almost reasonable the night before. But where had she come from, and where did she go? At no time had I felt threatened by the small, whimsical presence.

Who besides my aunt and Austin had known I was going to be at Laney's last night?

I gulped down a bowl of cereal while Aunt Nell buttoned the back of my blouse. As soon as I checked on Amanda's birth and death records, I planned to have a long, frank talk with my friend Austin Leatherwood.

"Slow down long enough to eat your breakfast!" My aunt pressed a glass of orange juice into my hand. "You won't get far on an empty stomach, and I need you to do a favor for me sometime today."

I obediently drained the glass as I wiggled into sandals. "What's that?"

"Will has outgrown his sneakers, and I'd planned to take him to the mall today, but I can't leave the house because I'm expecting a delivery."

"Sure, I'll take him this afternoon," I said. "but couldn't they just leave the delivery next door?"

She smiled. "Not this time."

"Why? What is it?" I asked.

"You'll find out," she said. "If you can be mysterious, Miss Laura, so can I."

"I'm not being mysterious," I argued. "I told you I was going to the courthouse, and I am."

She folded her arms. "I'm not talking about this morning, I'm talking about last night. You may have gotten those bites and scratches just walking Vesuvius, but I think there's more to it than that."

"We'll talk about it later!" I shouted on my way to the car. Maybe she would forget to ask.

But birth certificates weren't kept on file at the courthouse, I learned. They were at the health department next door, and the general public was not permitted to see them.

"Unless, of course, it's your own," Ethel Murchison took pleasure in informing me. She wore bright orchid lipstick and metallic green eyeshadow, and she walked as if her pantyhose were falling down. I wondered if she still blamed me for the time Laney and I "rolled" her yard one Halloween.

I tried not to let her know it was important to me. "Oh, well. Then the death certificates, could I—?"

"Those are in Columbia. You'll have to make an appointment to see them," she said with a triumphant gleam in her eyes. She turned to answer the phone, dismissing me with a casual wave of her hand, and I caught the eye of the young woman at the desk in the corner: Millie Butler. We had been high school flag girls together, and I remembered how as a greenhorn she had come to me for help in learning the routine. I was glad now I had given her a few hours of my time.

"Mrs. Murchison goes across the street for coffee in a few minutes," she whispered across the counter. "Stick around!"

I lurked about until I saw the woman leave, and then Millie quickly sneaked Amanda's birth certificate from the files. "Ordinarily I wouldn't," she confessed. "I could really get into trouble for this, but since this is someone who's been dead for years, I can't see what harm it will do.... But hurry, please!"

Thanking her, I read the document eagerly, certain I would find that Amanda was Ada Squires's daughter. But the record told me otherwise: Mary Amanda Scoggins, weighing seven pounds, four ounces, was born at home to Maxie and Jasper Scoggins on October 8, 1935. The certificate was signed by Dr. Walter P. Stanley, the same doctor who had delivered me, but who had died when I was a child.

Could there be two Mary Amandas? Dejected, I walked two blocks to *The Redpath Tribune*, the modest local newspaper published every Wednesday. Although it was still early, the heat steamed from the sidewalk, and I felt moisture trickling down my neck and under the once-crisp collar of my blouse.

Blakely Floyd and Austin's mother, Daisy Leatherwood, chatted amiably in front of The Gingham Apron, Blakely's latest venture. The ultrachic kitchenware shop featured utensils that few people in Redpath ever used and gadgets that many had never heard of. I gave it six months, give or take a week or so. Her clothing boutique had lasted a year, and her sandwich shop even less. It was a good thing Blakely's father had money because she usually got what she wanted, except Austin Leatherwood. And she hadn't given up on him.

"Laura!" Blakely called me over as she unlocked the door of her shop. I was glad to pause in the shade of the red-and-yellow-striped awning, where bright begonias filled wicker boxes on either side of the door. "I hope you're not still feeling the ill effects of your little adventure Saturday," she said. "We missed you at the picnic."

I'll bet, I thought, ignoring the door she held open for me. If a spider could smile, it would look just like her. "Thanks, but I'm fine," I assured her, in a hurry to move along.

But that was not to be. Daisy Leatherwood squeezed my hand. "Are you going to stay for the summer, dear?"

I smiled. "Well, for part of it anyway; I'm using Laney's car while they're doing some work on mine."

"I imagine your aunt is glad to have your help." Her tone was pleasant enough, but I was suddenly aware of my wilting attire, my floppy sandals, and the damp hair plastered to my forehead. "Give Nell my love, now.... Tell her to call me," she added as I left.

She meant well, I thought as I glanced back at the two of them. They were probably making plans to meet for lunch and renew their strategy on poor, vulnerable Austin, now that Laney was out of the way.

Had either of them had anything to do with what happened last night? Austin might have mentioned that I would be at Laney's, and Blakely was small enough to pass for a child in the dusk if she kept her distance. Still, I couldn't imagine her tramping through the fields at twilight. I smiled. I would have to look for someone with insect bites like mine.

Bailey Smith, the city editor of the *Tribune*, had graduated in the class before ours, so I had to spend half an hour telling him about everyone who had come to the class reunion before I could get to the files. I was relieved that he had to dash off for an interview before I was forced to explain the reason for my visit.

Alone in the small back room, I quickly found the edition I was looking for. The brief article about the child's death was almost lost in the news of Redpath's servicemen. Amanda had drowned when World War II was raging in Europe and the Pacific, and Redpath, South Carolina, like every other American town, was consumed by it.

Like the child, who had apparently been considered inconsequential, the story was small and insignificant and was squeezed in at the bottom of page one between a picture of those attending Bible school at the First Baptist Church and a notice about the next Red Cross meeting. The article read:

LOCAL CHILD DROWNS

Mary Amanda Scoggins, 7, daughter of Mr. and Mrs. Jasper Scoggins, Rt. 2, drowned Wed., July 14, in the Enoree River.

The child's body was discovered only a few yards

below Crybaby Bridge by Capt. Decatur Squires, who
was at home on furlough before leaving on an assign-
ment overseas.

Capt. Squires said the child had apparently been
playing on the bridge, which is near his home, and
had fallen into the water below. All efforts to resus-
citate her failed.

Services were held Fri. at Loganwood Chapel with
the Rev. Oliver Haynes officiating.

I slammed the dusty volume shut and walked into the
sun, glad to have it burning through my flimsy clothing,
making me warm again. No wonder the judge didn't want
to talk about Amanda! Had he seen her fall from the
bridge? Was he the one who pulled her from the water?
How hard had they tried to revive her? Was the distin-
guished Judge Decatur Squires holding something back?

And what about his grandson? I dialed Austin's office
as soon as I got home, but his secretary told me he would
be gone most of the day, so I left a message for him to call
me.

Gone where? I wondered. Was he conveniently dodg-
ing my call because he was afraid I had found out too
much? If so, why did he try to help me learn about
Amanda? My head ached, and when Will finally gave in
to his afternoon nap, I took two aspirin and a short rest.
My aunt didn't pursue the question of my evening adventures and insect bites, at least not yet; I was waiting for the
other shoe to fall.

When Will woke at three, Austin had still not returned
my call. Since Aunt Nell's mysterious delivery had not arrived, I took my small cousin for his new shoes. "Wed"
ones, he said. He was just beginning to talk, but he knew
his colors and insisted on red.

I dressed him proudly, buckled brown sandals onto his plump feet, and strapped him into his car seat. I had brushed his fine, yellow hair, and his face was clean—for a while, anyway—and he laughed and bounced, eager to be off. Being with him was like seeing life for the first time.

Because it was a Monday afternoon the mall wasn't crowded, but I soon regretted not bringing along Will's stroller. I would have enjoyed doing some window shopping, but it's difficult to browse carrying a sturdy two-year-old, so we went straight to the shoe department at Belk's, where Will was fitted with his new "wed" shoes. The brown sandals went in a box to take home.

Since it was still early, I took him for a ride on the escalator and bought him a teddy bear from the toy department. "Will you be my teddy bear, Will?" I asked. "Will you be Laura's bear?"

"I Dauwa's beah," he said, allowing me a quick hug, and I know I fairly glowed with pride. I must have looked like a fool, but I didn't care. How was I ever going to leave this child?

The department store was an unusually large one for a town the size of Redpath because the mall was several miles from town and was shared by several communities. Still, I never went there without seeing someone I knew, and this time was no exception.

"Laura Graham! Over here!" A tall girl with an armful of packages waved at me from the perfume counter as Will and I descended to the main floor for the third time, Will being fascinated with the ride.

"I keep trying to get your attention, and you keep getting back on the escalator," she said. "Is this a marathon or something?"

Her name clicked into place. Judy. Judy Gregg had lived in my dorm for the first two years of college and had later transferred to another school. I hadn't seen her in years.

"Judy Fraser now," she said, displaying a dainty daughter asleep in her stroller. "Is this yours?" she asked as Will tugged at my hand.

How fortunate I felt to be able to show him off! "I wish he were," I said, and explained the situation.

"Oh, not Laney!" she whispered. "I didn't know, I'm so sorry." She smiled at Will. "He's beautiful."

I couldn't argue. "Let's get some ice cream," I suggested. "I promised Will a treat, and it will give us a chance to catch up on things."

Will insisted on walking as we moved out into the mall, and I didn't argue since my arms were almost numb. I let him romp in front of us, keeping an eye on him as we stopped from time to time to look at window displays.

Later, I was to scold myself a million times. I only turned my head a minute, but that was all the time it took, and when I looked up, he was gone.

Will had been fascinated by a fountain in the center of the mall, and as we paused to look at it, Judy's baby woke, and her crying was not delicate at all. I had glanced at Will, still entranced by the splashing fountain, and since it was surrounded by a metal railing, I had thought he couldn't possibly fall in. I took Judy's packages and held them while she comforted her daughter and found a bottle of orange juice to keep her happy.

As I said, it only took a minute, but it was a minute I would remember for the rest of my life. The shock of not seeing him there awakened nerves I didn't even know I had, and I looked frantically about while bargaining subconsciously with the Deity to please let me find him again.

"Will! Where's Will!" I circled the fountain, looking for a blond toddler with a brown bear. "He's gone! He was right here, and he's gone!" My voice rose. People began to stare. I didn't care.

"Laura, he can't have gone far." Judy's voice was steady. He wasn't her child. "Come on," she said, "we'll find him."

"Have you seen a tiny boy in blue shorts and a white shirt?" I asked every shopper I met. "He was wearing new red shoes." No one had seen him, but almost everyone I asked joined in the search.

My head felt as if it were about to explode and I wanted to burst into tears, but I didn't deserve to cry. I didn't deserve to have Will's love, to have him hug me and call me "Dauwa." And Aunt Nell, who had just lost the person dearest to her—what was I going to tell her?

Judy and I dashed in a frenzy from store to store, searching, asking, but still no Will. It seemed as if he had been lost for an eternity. "I'm going to call the security guard," I said, wondering why I hadn't had sense enough to think of that before. "They'll know what to do."

"Ma'am?" A teenage boy approached me. There was an undercurrent of excitement in his voice. "That little boy you're looking for . . . well, there's a man in the pet shop down there with a little kid holding a teddy, just like—"

"Oh, God! Where?" I didn't know whether to laugh or cry.

"The pet shop, right there on the corner!" He pointed.

Later, I remembered that I didn't even take time to thank him but went racing into the little shop like a crazy person and came to a stumbling halt just inside the door.

Will stood at the back of the store contentedly holding a strange man's hand and laughing at the kittens on display. "Kitty! See kitty!" He held his teddy up to "see," and the man who was with him laughed and tousled his hair—*tousled his hair as if he had a right to!*

My legs went weak. I couldn't see his face, but the man seemed familiar. I had seen him before, but where? I felt sick. I had heard about these people, horrible people who kidnapped innocent children and did unspeakable things. The man must be stopped! I would grab Will and run, but the man must not be allowed to go free. I turned to the clerk. "*Please*, call the—"

"Dauwa!" Little Will came running, laughing into my arms, and the man slowly followed. He didn't try to get away but stood there waiting and smiling as if nothing had happened. And then I saw his face.

"Why, you're the vet! You're—you're, uh—Marshall Sidney!"

He grinned. "Sidney Marshall. Everyone gets it backwards."

I clutched Will to me and backed away. Realization hit me like a bucket of well water. "You've been following us, haven't you? You're the one who was behind me the other night? You scared me to death! Why?"

His smile vanished. "Maybe I should remind you that I found Will walking down the mall this afternoon with no one but a bear for company and no sign of you." The man's voice was low and calm, but his eyes were threatening. "You'd better be grateful I was keeping an eye on him."

I looked around. A concerned crowd had gathered. "It's all right," I told them. "This gentleman found him, and he's fine. Thank you, everything's fine."

But was it? "Don't go away, please," I whispered to Judy. "Just stick around while I work this out, okay?"

She nodded mutely, probably wondering what she'd gotten herself into and swearing to avoid me in the future.

Sidney Marshall insisted on buying Will the promised ice cream, and we wandered out to benches in the mall. "Tell me why you've been following us," I demanded. "What do you want? Who are you?"

He stroked his beard. "Look, I'll admit I've been trying to speak with you. Your aunt won't let me get close to her, won't even talk with me on the phone. I thought I could reason with you."

"About what?" I looked at him closely. "What do you want?"

He sighed. "I want my son, Laura. I thought your aunt had told you. I'm Will's father."

SEVENTEEN

THERE WAS NO DOUBT in my mind that Sidney Marshall was telling the truth. The shape of Will's face and the way his hair grew back from his forehead were very much like his father's. Sidney held his son on one knee, the bear on the other. They reminded me of a figurine carved from warm-grained wood.

"You're a long time announcing yourself," I said.

"I didn't know," he told me. "Your aunt doesn't believe me, won't even give me a chance to explain, but the first time I learned about Will was back in January, when I came home from the Peace Corps."

"But surely Laney would—"

He interrupted me with a wave of his hand. "Nothing was sure about Laney. Don't you know that by now?"

"Still, it's hard to believe she wouldn't tell you she was pregnant with your child," I insisted.

"To tell you the truth, I doubt if she knew it when I left," he said, wiping a trail of chocolate from Will's chin. "Look, I was in love with Laney; in a way I guess I always will be, and this little fellow is all I have left: a part of her, and a part of me...." His voice was choked with emotion. "Can't you understand why I want him?"

I nodded silently. Across the mall I watched Judy Fraser wheel her baby out of a dress shop and pause momentarily with a question in her eyes. I smiled and waved, dismissing her. She seemed relieved.

"Laney and I had a bitter disagreement in October of that year," Sidney continued. "I had graduated the summer before and applied to the Peace Corps. Then I met Laney." He smiled, sliding Will down his leg to ride his foot like a horse. "Love hit me like a tornado, picked me up, and swept me into never-never land. I think Laney loved me, too, but she had another two years of vet school. I wanted to marry then; she didn't, and I gave her an ultimatum."

Sidney Marshall shook his head. "I was a fool, and just to spite her I started seeing someone else. Then shortly after that, I was accepted into the Peace Corps and left in November for Africa. It was an impulsive decision that I've since regretted—not my service in Africa, but the way I left Laney." He shrugged. "She never answered my letters, and of course when I came home and tried to look her up, I learned about Will." He swung the squealing child in the air, then planted a kiss on his cheek. "I knew he was mine," he said. "I've missed almost two years of my child's life. Two years! And if I hadn't loved Laney, hadn't kept on caring, I might never have learned I had a son at all." His eyes weren't laughing anymore. "I haven't forgiven Laney for that. I don't know if I ever will."

I took Will's small, warm hand in mine, and slowly the icy lump in my stomach disappeared. Could this loving, apparently gentle man have had anything to do with my cousin's death?

"What took you so long to find her?" I asked. "You must have known to look here first."

He turned away. "Your aunt lied to me, told me she wasn't here, that she was living on the West Coast." His fingers knotted into a fist. The bear fell to the floor unheeded. "She sent me on a wild-goose chase." He shrugged. "Why?"

"Buying time." I spoke without thinking. "Buying time for Laney." I wondered why. "Did you find her, talk with her before...?"

Will was becoming tired and fretful, so we rose and walked through the mall with the child between us, looking much like any young family out for an afternoon stroll. I glanced at our reflection in a store window and almost didn't recognize myself.

"I talked with Laney twice, both times by phone," he said finally. "She tried to tell me Will wasn't mine!" His laugh was harsh. "As if I couldn't count! She must have thought I'd left knowing about the baby, that I'd deliberately hurt her, and now she was hurting me back."

Sidney swung Will onto his shoulders in one easy motion as we walked onto the hot asphalt of the parking lot. "And then I heard she was seeing that guy again, her high school sweetheart, Austin what's-his-name, and I was afraid she'd marry him and that would be that. I'd never see my son again."

And that was exactly what Laney intended to do, I thought, and I realized why my cousin had come home to practice in Redpath. She probably hadn't counted on the child's father following her here filled with hurt and rejection and the driving need to claim his son.

One solid push from a very high place could have filled that need, I thought. But had it?

EIGHTEEN

"YOU'RE ONLY MAKING things worse," I said to my aunt. "If Sidney Marshall can prove he's Will's father, we might never see the child again if you persist in turning the man away! Do you want this thing dragged through the courts, plastered all over the newspapers? At least give him a chance to explain."

If Sidney Marshall had anything to do with Laney's death, I wanted to know about it now, not when it might be too late.

I was aware of a rising edge to my voice, but I couldn't help it. I had never realized Aunt Nell could be so inflexible, so pigheaded. The little I had seen of Sidney Marshall led me to believe that if crossed, he could be a vengeful man, but I couldn't seem to convince my aunt of the consequences.

I had persuaded the young vet to wait until the next day before trying again to contact my aunt. "Give me a few hours to soften her up," I said. But now it seemed as if it might take a few years.

She had met Will and me at the door that day, all smiling and mysterious, with an air of excitement about her, and it didn't take Will long to find out what it was all about. The department store had delivered his birthday present a few weeks early, and it beckoned with circus brilliance from the far corner of the backyard. A gym set, red and white like a peppermint stick, with two swings, a slide and a trapeze bar, was anchored to the ground with a look of permanence. My aunt meant for the gym set to stay, and for Will to stay with it. A rope swing would have been much easier to deal with.

Later, after Will finally gave in to sleep, my aunt and I took our light supper out to the front porch, where again I brought up the subject of Will's father.

"I'm not even sure he is Will's father," she said. Her reaction wasn't as impassioned as before, but there was a slight tremor in her voice.

"Have you looked at him?" I asked. "And he was at school with Laney. I'm sure we could get in touch with some of their classmates and find out the details, but I don't think there's much doubt about it."

Silence. "Even so," she said at last, "he had no business leaving her, going off to who knows where, and poor Laney carrying his child!"

"Aunt Nell, he didn't know," I said. I felt like a defense lawyer pleading a case, with my aunt as judge and jury. "Laney never told him."

"Humph! So *he* says!"

Still, I felt she had softened just a bit, and when she got up to go inside, I couldn't resist one last pitch. "Aunt Nell, that man is hurting as much as you and I, maybe even more." The screen door slammed on her silence.

But my aunt's conscience must have worked on her during the night, because the next morning she announced with a significant look at Will, "If *that man* calls again today, you may tell him to come by this afternoon, but I don't want the baby here when he comes."

"Maybe you're right," I said, filling a large water bowl for Vesuvius. The two of them needed to be alone to work things out together. "We'll take the dog for a walk—that is, if I can pry this child away from that swing set." I smiled as Will darted out the door with his breakfast half-eaten and a bib still flapping around his neck.

At least this time I wouldn't be followed on my walk around town, I thought with relief. And maybe I would pay another call on Mr. Nevin at the library.

"Aunt Nell," I asked, trailing behind her as she hurried after Will, "do you remember when Nevin Squires was in the hospital last winter?"

Hastily she swiped at the child's grubby face with a damp cloth and untied the bib before allowing him to squirm free. "As a matter of fact, I do. It was just before Valentine's Day, because several of us sent him flowers, red and white carnations with a big, heart-shaped lollipop right in the middle." My aunt walked slowly back inside and poured another cup of coffee from the pot on the stove. "You know, I've always liked Nevin; he's a timid sort, but that's his papa's doing." She smiled. "And he's good to let me know when something I like comes in. He knows what I like to read."

"How long was he sick?" I asked. "Was it anything serious?"

She frowned. "Well, I'm sure it was painful. Daisy said it was kidney stones. Of course, Nevin would never talk about it, prim as he is!" Aunt Nell cast a reassuring glance at Will out the kitchen window. "I don't think they kept him more than a few days. You know how they are now— toss you out when you're half dead! But we wanted to do something nice for him. Nevin doesn't have a whole lot of friends, so some of us went in together and sent the Valentine arrangement. He seemed to appreciate it, sent a lovely note."

I smiled. According to my aunt, many of the world's problems could be solved if only someone took the time to write a "lovely note."

"And he was only out for about a week?" I asked, trying to maintain a casual tone.

"Probably less than that. I don't think he missed more than three or four days at the library." She folded her arms and looked at me. "Why?"

I quickly began stacking the breakfast dishes. "Why? Because I heard he'd been sick, and I was afraid it might be something serious, that's why! Can't I care about him, too?"

I really didn't intend to get carried away with my indignant reply, but it seemed to work. My aunt backed off with a flustered apology, leaving me with a tinge of guilt for my devious behavior.

And I was fond of Mr. Nevin, but why had he lied about talking with Laney? I was almost certain he had told me he was in the hospital for a few weeks just before my cousin died, when in fact he had only missed several days of work. Upstairs, I looked again at the notice he had sent Laney. The book that was overdue was a collection of poetry by Sylvia Plath.

Why should that surprise me? Laney had chosen the poet as the subject of her high school term paper, but I remembered her frantic, last-minute research, her dire mutterings: "I'll never read Sylvia Plath again...sick of her...wish I'd never heard of the silly woman!"

Of course I'd felt the same way at the time about Edna St. Vincent Millay, but I had mellowed since and relented. It was somehow reassuring to read the familiar words again. Maybe Laney had changed her mind about the works of Sylvia Plath.

I tucked the printed reminder, along with Amanda's locket and the pitiful threadbare lamb, into a shoebox and shoved them out of sight on my closet shelf. They had seemed so vulnerable tossed in with the contents of my dresser drawer, jumbled with stray earrings and half-used bottles of cologne.

I would bring my doubts into the open and ask Nevin Squires about the card. I was certain he would have a reasonable explanation.

But the nearer we came to the library that afternoon, the more dubious I became. Nevin Squires was a longtime family friend. What if he realized I suspected him of lying—or worse?

I had left my aunt nervously plucking out stitches in the pillow cover she was making for Will. It was a cross-stitch sampler of Little Boy Blue, and she had unwittingly stitched in two extra rows of "corn." "It's all that man's fault!" she grumbled. "I'm all jumblethumbs, Laura. What am I going to say to him?"

"Don't worry, you'll work it out," I said, hoping it was true. I had called Sidney Marshall and invited him to come at three. When I left with Will in his stroller and Vesuvius trotting amiably behind a few minutes before he was due, Aunt Nell stood on the front porch and watched us all the way down the street. I hated the grief and fear in her face, and just then I hated Sidney Marshall for contributing to it.

Mr. Nevin smiled when he saw us and took Will in his arms to the preschool section, where Will sat in a little red rocking chair and looked at fuzzy animal books. "Well now, Miss Laura," Mr. Nevin said. "What great truths are you seeking today?"

I felt the blood rush to my face. Could the man read my thoughts? But he was joking, of course. "I can't stay," I said. "I left my dog out front. But in packing Laney's things I found an overdue book reminder, and I just wanted to see if it was returned."

He looked at me expectantly. I seemed to be running out of breath.

"A collection of Sylvia Plath's works," I gasped, pretending to be interested in *The Farm's ABC Book* that Will had thrust in my face.

"Oh yes, I'm sure that was returned," he said, smiling faintly. "Unfortunately, there's not much call for it, though."

"Then Laney must have brought it back," I said.

But he was not to be tricked. "Very possibly your aunt did. Your cousin didn't have a lot of free time, so Nell did some of her errands for her." His words were slow and patient as always. Did he suspect my motives?

"I was a little surprised at her choice of reading material," I explained. "She seldom read poetry unless she had to, and when Laney read anything at all, it was something like a Dorothy Sayers mystery. She loved a Lord Peter Whimsey, loved the humor in them, remember?"

He nodded, his eyes clouding. "Well now, Laney did like a good puzzle and a good joke. But sometimes people change, Laura." He sighed. "That's human nature."

I looked straight into the small dwarf marigold in his lapel: gold, edged with bronze. "Yes," I said, "I guess you're right."

I remembered an old television commercial for margarine. "It's not nice to fool Mother Nature," it warned. Human nature could be dangerous, too. Was I pushing someone too far? Had Laney?

I had expected the librarian to have a logical explanation for Laney's returning the book, and he had. Why had I not asked him about the message he had written at the bottom of the card offering to take the book back for her? *Because that would be going too far!* Besides, the poor man had probably forgotten all about it, and I was being ridiculous.

At the corner store I treated the three of us, including the dog, to ice cream, then stopped for a short visit with Ginny Adair. We took the long way home by way of the school playground just to give my aunt and Sidney Marshall the time they needed to be alone. I halfway expected angry, raised voices to greet us through the open windows when we trudged wearily up the walk on our return, but to my surprise the house was silent. The young vet's car was not in the driveway, and neither was Aunt Nell's.

"Gone to store, be right back" was the message scribbled on the note pad by the door, and the mail waited, ignored, in the box where the postman had left it earlier.

I turned both of my charges loose in the backyard and sat on the steps to see if there was a letter from Spencer. There wasn't, but then, I had only been gone a week, and I hadn't written to him, either.

But there was something addressed to me, typed on a business-size envelope and postmarked Bishopville, South Carolina. I frowned. Who did I know in Bishopville? When I drew out the slip of paper, I felt as though a blast of winter air blew through me on the sun-warmed steps. The message contained only three words:

Don't forget Amanda!

The handwriting was Laney's.

NINETEEN

I PLACED THE SCRAP of paper on the steps, then stood and backed away as if it were a poisonous spider. If this was someone's idea of a joke, it was a cruel thing to do, and I couldn't imagine anyone in Redpath sadistic enough to even think of such a thing.

The familiar handwriting almost jumped at me. If it hadn't been written by Laney, the note had been copied by someone who knew my cousin's hurried style.

I snatched up the letter at the sound of my aunt's car in the driveway. She must never know this had come, this taunting bit of hope supposedly from someone whose broken body had washed ashore below Crybaby Bridge. The local rescue squad had found her; Aunt Nell had identified her body. My cousin Laney was dead. Wasn't she?

I hurt. The pain tore at me, shrieked through my body. I stuffed the letter into my handbag and ran to the sink to dash cold water on my face. I could hide the note, but I couldn't hide my tears. It was useless to try.

"Laura, Will, I'm home!" My aunt's voice was steady; she smiled as she came in the door. "Well, we—*Laura!* What on earth is wrong? Is it Will? Is he—"

Her fear seemed to melt as I showed her the child playing happily on his swing set.

"I'm sorry, it just came over me all of a sudden," I said. "I guess I was worried about this afternoon, about you and Sidney." I wiped my eyes with a paper towel and tried to smile. "How did it go?"

She put an arm around me and pushed me gently into a kitchen chair. I heard her filling the kettle for tea. "Well, you can relax. It went very well. And you're right, he is Will's father; he really cares about that child. Sidney Marshall knows it would be disastrous to unsettle Will now, to snatch him away."

She sat across from me, and placed her hand over mine. "We'll have to see that it's legal, of course. I've made an appointment with a lawyer; I insisted on that, and he wanted it, too. I'm convinced he wants what's best for Will, and so do I. After all, I'm not a young woman anymore, and I have to consider the child's future."

I sighed. I didn't mean to; it just escaped me. I was glad for Will, and yet I wasn't. "How long . . . ?"

Aunt Nell shrugged. "Sidney has decided to stay on here, to accept Bill Ratteree's offer. He can visit Will here whenever he likes and eventually have him for weekends; of course he plans to contribute to his support." She frowned. "One of these days I suppose he'll find someone else and marry. Until then, I'll just take each day as it comes and try to get the most from it." My aunt squeezed my hand as she rose to pour steaming water into the pot. "I've learned to do that, Laura. You must learn to, too. Remember what Laney said: 'Don't wait too long at the fair.'"

We both jumped when the phone rang, and my aunt's hand flew to her mouth. "Oh, in all the excitement I forgot to tell you. Austin Leatherwood called you yesterday and again this afternoon. I guess he thinks I'm deliberately not giving you the messages."

I smiled. Austin. I could share my worries with Austin. Eagerly I raced for the phone. It seemed like weeks since I had seen him.

But it wasn't Austin Leatherwood on the line. "Laura! Just checking in, hon. How's it going?" Spencer's voice seemed strained. "When can I look for you home? Aren't they through with your car yet?"

"The car should be ready in a few days, Spence," I said. "But to tell you the truth, I won't." I lowered my voice. "This is going to take some time."

He hesitated. "I miss you, Laura. What if I drive up this weekend? We can go out to dinner, see a show or something."

"I don't think so, Spencer. Just give me a little more time. Please?"

"Time for what? What's wrong, Laura?"

I swallowed. How could I say it? "It's hard to explain over the phone. I'll write, Spence."

"You do that!" He slammed the receiver down so hard, it hurt my ear. He was furious, and I didn't blame him. Spencer Gaines was a good friend; he loved me, and I had hurt him. I sniffed. Sometimes life was just plain rotten! Then I thought of Austin waiting for my call...and sometimes life wasn't so bad.

"I need to see you," I said when Austin finally answered his phone. "It's urgent."

"Well," he drawled, "sounds promising!" There was laughter in his voice, and it irritated me. It was odd that his sense of humor, the very thing that attracted me to him, should annoy me so at times.

And I was attracted to Austin Leatherwood. I could no longer deny it, not even to myself. And I was having a hell of a time trying to hide it as we drove aimlessly in circles that evening with a bucket of chicken between us.

"Will you please park this thing somewhere?" I growled. "I'm getting dizzy!" I inhaled the fragrance of the chicken, which blended with the doggy odor of the truck's interior. It wasn't a bad combination.

"Well, what do you think?" I bit into a drumstick as we pulled into a roadside picnic spot a few miles from town.

Austin studied the note I had given him earlier. "It does look like Laney's writing, but it can't be, Laura. This thing's postmarked yesterday."

I stared at him without speaking, then looked quickly out the window.

"Laney is dead, Laura. This can't be from Laney."

"Did you see her?" I asked. "Are you sure it was Laney?"

He shook his head. "Your Aunt Nell saw her, and there were dental records, jewelry—how could it possibly be anyone else?"

The bite of chicken went down like a rock. I wasn't hungry anymore. "But the note! Who sent it? Why?"

He shoved impatiently at the visor as the late evening sun slanted into his face. "I don't know. That's what we have to find out." Austin examined the postmark. "Bishopville. I've never been there. I don't know anybody who lives there."

"Neither do I," I said.

"I guess the first thing to do is check and see if somebody's living there using her name," he said, digging for the right piece of chicken. "The whole thing is weird, it's creepy."

"That's not the half of it," I told him, relating my adventures in his family cemetery, "and this time I have the musical lamb to prove it."

We carried our supper to the picnic table and brushed off the weatherstained benches. Austin was having problems absorbing this tidbit of information. It's not every day someone calmly announces they've seen a ghost. "I saw her, Austin," I repeated. "I'm not making it up. I saw Amanda."

"You saw someone in a white dress," he said. "That's all."

"Then who?" I asked. "And why?"

He stood and paced in the small cleared area behind the table. "I don't know. I've heard of Aunt Ada from Mother; she remembers when she died. And I've seen the small grave with the lamb on it." He rested against a tulip poplar; its leaves cast his lean face in shadow. "Once I asked Uncle Nevin who was buried there. You know how morbid young children sometimes are, and I wanted to know the story behind it."

"And what did he say?"

"Not much. Said he thought she was a child of some tenants. Aunt Delia always looked after her grave, just as she looked after the others. I never thought any more about it."

"Something worries me about your Uncle Nevin," I admitted, and I told him about finding the library notice.

"Laura, you know how absent-minded Uncle Nevin is," he reminded me. "He probably doesn't even remember sending that card." His voice was short and curt, and I knew he was annoyed with me, yet I had to share my doubt with someone.

"But why would he lie to me about how long he stayed in the hospital?" I asked.

"I can't believe you!" With much wrenching and straining, he jerked open the dented door on the passenger side of the truck. "You sound like you suspect Uncle Nevin of something awful! You've known him all your life, Laura Graham, and a kinder person never lived!"

I had never seen anyone sputter so. I made a broad gesture of wiping the spittle from my face with a paper nap-

kin and wringing it out. Then I leaned against the faded
blue fender of the truck and laughed until the tears ran.

Austin watched me, frowning, with folded arms, but the
corners of his mouth quivered. "You're a funny one,
Laura," he said, swinging me into the truck. My waist felt
warm where his big hands had held me. "Tell you what,"
he said. "First thing tomorrow, I'll call over to Bishopville, see what I can find out."

"*We'll* call," I said. "After all, I was the one who got
the note."

He slid into the seat beside me and briefly touched my
cheek with his fingers. "We'll call," he said with a grin.
"I'll swear, Laura, sometimes you remind me of Laney."

I pulled away from him and clicked my seat belt into
place. I wanted to go home and sleep without dreaming.
It had been a long, long day, and I felt as if my emotions
had gone down the river without a raft.

TWENTY

AUSTIN RAN A PENCIL slowly down the page and circled a section in red. "Here are the real estate firms listed for Bishopville," he said, glancing up at me. "Maybe one of them has sold or rented a place to someone using Laney's name."

We sat in his small back office in his father's real estate and insurance firm. Most of the space was occupied by a large gun-metal-colored desk and a filing cabinet, leaving barely enough room for two chairs.

I shifted on mine and glanced through the window into the next room where one salesman typed into a computer and another talked over the phone. I had only been there fifteen minutes and already I was getting claustrophobia. But fifteen minutes was all it took to phone the post office, the city hall, and the small town's one motel. No one had ever heard of Laney McCall. I really hadn't expected them to.

Austin shook his head after speaking with the last person on his list and stood, reaching for his coat. "No luck. Come on, let's get out of here. I'll buy us a hot dog."

I was only too ready to follow.

It was just past noon, and the tiny lunchroom on Main Street was crowded. After a few minutes of waiting, Austin and I found places at the counter and ordered our lunch. Several young women who clerked at the courthouse stared at us as we came in, and I heard laughter from their table in the corner. I felt my face getting warm and was irritated with myself for being so touchy. For all I knew, they were only telling jokes.

Lettie's Lunchroom was not a place for intimate exchanges. The main topics of conversation, which seemed to run in ripples from front to back, were the dry weather, the best way to make peach ice cream, and whether or not Myra Sue Shumaker's second husband had or had not played tackle for the Redpath High School Fighting Warriors.

Lettie herself refereed, filling orders from time to time. The hot dog was delicious.

Austin dipped his last french fry in ketchup and folded it into his mouth. "I really don't see any need to drive over there," he said, wadding his napkin into a ball. "We'd have to have someone on permanent duty at the post office, and they still might never show."

"Or they could have been just passing through," I said as we walked outside into a blast of midday heat. "I can't imagine why anybody would do a thing like this, but I have a feeling we haven't heard the last of them."

Austin was silent as he walked with me to my car. "It's almost as though someone's teasing us with pieces of a puzzle." He paused in the shade of a storefront awning with a strange expression on his face. "I have the most peculiar notion that someone is sitting back pulling the strings and laughing as we jump. It almost sounds like something—" Austin looked at his watch and broke into a run. "I'm sorry, Laura, gotta rush! I'm supposed to show a house at one."

I thought about what Austin had almost said as I drove back to Aunt Nell's. He hadn't completed his sentence, but I knew what he was going to say: *It almost sounds like something Laney would do.*

I parked my cousin's Volkswagen in what little shade I could find and went inside, looking for something to do. I found it.

While Will and Aunt Nell napped, I cleaned both bathrooms and mopped the kitchen floor; and later, after everyone woke, I sat down for a challenging workout at the piano. I had been playing some almost every day while at Aunt Nell's, and a few practices from my earlier training had come back to me. I was annoyed with myself for not keeping up with something that meant so much to me, and made a silent promise to make up for it.

The demanding discipline of music gave me a brief respite of peace, but I couldn't erase the nagging apprehension over the note from Bishopville, and later that day when the long afternoon shadows gave an illusion of coolness, I trudged behind the lawnmower, crossing back and forth on the small rectangle of grass in front of the house. There was a sense of order in rigidly trimming each narrow strip and raking away the cuttings until the yard was neat and uncluttered, and as I worked I thought of Laney.

I remembered how my cousin was always the first to suggest a scavenger or treasure hunt, and how in our early teens we often competed in a nocturnal diversion called Fox and Hounds. The game was usually played in the summer and fall and involved a group of players with flashlights (the hounds) following chalk arrows left by one person with a head start (the fox), who tried to get back to base without getting caught. It sometimes covered the entire town of Redpath.

We had played Fox and Hounds at nearly every party, and even at our church youth group, for two years in a row until Alvin Burkhalter ran into the barbed-wire fence behind Catoe's chicken lot and had to have ten stitches and a tetanus shot. When our parents made us stop playing, Laney wouldn't go to youth group anymore, and she refused to have anything else to do with Alvin Burkhalter, although I don't suppose he cared.

I could almost hear my cousin's laughing, see her sprinting back to base all red-faced and sweating with those long, tan legs giving her an edge over the trailing "hounds."

I pushed the lawnmower into the shed and went inside to wash my hands for supper. I had worked up an appetite for the ham that had been baking all afternoon. But there was no food on the table, and I found my aunt in the steamy downstairs bathroom trying to plaster Will's stubborn cowlick with water.

She glanced at me in agitation. "I give up! It will just have to do. We're late already."

I started. "Late to what?"

"The Women of the Church are having their covered dish supper tonight." Aunt Nell gave the soft yellow hair one more lick with the brush. "You know we always meet on the third Wednesday, Laura! I just assumed you weren't planning to go when you started mowing the lawn so late." She paused. "We can wait if you'll hurry."

I glanced at my dirty shorts. Bits of grass stuck to my legs, and my shirt was streaked with grease. "Thanks, but I'll pass this time," I said.

"Will's had his supper," my aunt told me, "but since they're providing a nursery, I thought I'd take him along. It will give you time to rest and Will a chance to play with the others."

I nodded mutely as they hurried out the door. "There's ham in the refrigerator," she called.

It didn't take me long to find it. I concocted a large garden salad and a gigantic ham sandwich and wolfed them

down with two tall glasses of milk. For dessert my aunt
had left two gooey, nut-filled brownies that practically
oozed calories, but I had already put on weight since I'd
been there. I didn't need any more to eat.

I polished off one standing at the sink and the other on
my way upstairs. I looked forward to a long, hot shower
and a few relaxing hours with a good book. Aunt Nell had
just finished the latest best-seller, and I was eager to begin
it. It waited in all its spectacular glory on my bedside table.

I had just stepped into the shower when I heard the
phone ring. I wondered if all telephones were made with a
sneaky little gadget that caused them to jingle demand-
ingly the minute you turned on the tap. Well, if the message was important, whoever it was would call back, I
thought.

A few minutes later, tingling pleasantly and smelling of
exotic flowers, I roughly toweled myself dry and was running a comb through my wet hair when I thought I heard
a footstep in the hall outside the bathroom door. Surely the
church supper wasn't over yet. My aunt had only been
gone a little over an hour, and I knew they usually had a
program after the meal.

"Aunt Nell," I called, "is anything wrong? Is something the matter with Will?"

No one answered. I started to open the door, then
thought better of it. Instead I clicked the latch into place
and called again, this time louder. Still no answer. If
someone else were inside the house, it wasn't my aunt. I
tried to remember if I had locked the doors before coming
upstairs. I had been so intent on stuffing myself with
brownies, I hadn't thought to check the locks. For all I
knew, both front and back doors were open to the public:
Come on in and help yourself!

I slipped into a brief nightshirt and a light robe that hung on the back of the door and looked around for a weapon. I had my choice of a toilet brush and a large plastic bottle of mouthwash. Why did everything come in namby-pamby plastic containers, I thought, when I desperately needed a heavy, menacing piece of glass?

I snatched up the wastebasket and clasped it to me, a flimsy wicker token of defense, but if whoever was out there tried to come in, I could cram it over his head and perhaps blind him long enough to get away. At the same time, I might even poke him in the stomach with the toilet brush. I almost smiled. Any other time it would have been funny. But it wasn't funny. Here I stood, half-naked and defenseless against whoever crept about on the other side of the flimsy wooden door.

I switched off the light and listened, standing stiffly behind the door, the Formica edge of the vanity cutting into my thighs. The small space was not meant for me, my wastebasket, and my toilet brush. There were too many molecules trying to occupy the same area, and it occurred to me I might even be breaking a law of physics. Laney would be pleased. She hated physics.

I tried not to make too much noise breathing, although if someone were out there, they certainly knew of my presence by now. But I didn't hear any more movement in the hall.

Where on earth was Vesuvius, and why hadn't he barked? Aunt Nell wouldn't allow him past the kitchen, and he usually slept on the back porch by the door, so that anyone who wanted to go outside had to step over him. I was almost certain our intruder had come boldly in the front.

And then I heard the stairs creak—not once, but twice. An old house settling as the evening air cooled, or a bur-

glar descending the steps? I hoped he would leave before
Aunt Nell and Will returned. I shifted to the edge of the
tub, thinking of the consequences of such an event. The
two of them would come in boldly, unsuspecting, and the
surprised trespasser would react—how? Perhaps vio-
lently, without thinking.

No light showed beneath the door. Thank goodness I
hadn't turned one on in the hall. Surely it must be dark
outside by now. Had I left a lamp burning in the living
room? I didn't think so; it had still been light when I came
upstairs. Would my aunt think it odd to return to a dark
house and decide to go for help? Probably not.

I waited and listened, still clutching my wastebasket.
Minutes passed. Surely whoever had been in the house, if
anyone had indeed come inside, had left by now. But if
not, my aunt and my small cousin were vulnerable to
whatever might happen. I had to warn them.

I abandoned my wastebasket for a can of spray deodorant that I remembered seeing on the back of the toilet tank
and quietly unlocked the door.

The hall was black and silent. My hair dripped on my
shoulders as I stepped onto the smooth hardwood floor
and I shivered, even though the night was warm. Sliding
soundlessly on bare feet, I moved with my back against the
wall, stepped quickly past the dark, open doorway of the
room where I slept, and inched my way down the stairs.

The house was dark except for a faint yellow glow from
the streetlight. I gripped the banister with a moist hand,
afraid to go forward and even more reluctant to look over
my shoulder. If Aunt Nell were to come home now, she
would probably smile to see me crouching alone on the dim
stairs.

"Laura, you're not getting enough rest," she would say.
"You're much too jumpy. Don't you know old houses pop

and creak a little at night?'' And of course she would be right.

I let out my breath in one long, easy sigh and moved on down the stairs. Too late, I saw the shadow on the landing. Someone had been hiding, waiting in the narrow window niche where the stairs turned. Now that someone moved when I did, and we did a funny little dance competing for the same space.

Physics again. The dark form pushed past me, and I fell backward as a firm shoulder bumped against mine. The can of deodorant dropped from my hand and clattered down the stairs.

I sat on a step and rubbed my forehead where it had collided with the bannister while the intruder ran down the steps and outside. I didn't yell ''Stop'' or ''Come back'' or ''Wait,'' as you hear victims do on television. I just wanted my mysterious visitor to get the hell out and leave me alone!

TWENTY-ONE

THE SCREEN DOOR bounced, and the sound of running feet pounded across the front porch. I heard Vesuvius bark sharply from the kitchen door and the sound of his toenails click against the wood as he ran down the back steps.

"Now you warn me," I muttered, switching on a light in the downstairs hall. Outside I heard him pawing the back gate, whining to be let out. I thought briefly of letting him have a go at it, but I wasn't sure our prowler didn't have a gun.

I opened the kitchen door to let him in. As useless as he was, I would still feel more secure just having the bulk of him about. And then I saw the ham bone on the back steps. No wonder he hadn't barked earlier: he had been happily gnawing on one of his favorite goodies. Aunt Nell must not be planning to make bean soup this time, I thought. She would have saved the ham bone for that. "Senate soup," she called it.

On impulse I glanced in the refrigerator. There, on the bottom shelf, wrapped tightly in foil, was the large, meaty bone from tonight's meal. My aunt hadn't given Vesuvius the bone; someone else had given him one, someone who wanted to keep him quiet.

I remembered the phone ringing while I was in the shower. My shadowy intruder had checked first to see if anyone was at home. It was common knowledge to everyone in Redpath that my aunt usually attended the covered-dish suppers at the church each month, but our burglar wasn't taking chances.

The silly dog pounced about, ecstatic over being allowed past his usual limits, and sniffed suspiciously around the front door, pausing to give a brief token growl.

"Why didn't you do that before?" I complained. And then I remembered something I had almost forgotten in the frenzy of being shoved on the stairs. I had detected a definite fragrance when the intruder pushed past me. I sniffed, moving slowly up the steps. It was faint, but it was still there: a sweet summer smell; it reminded me of sticky stovetops and pans of simmering fruit. Strawberries! My nocturnal visitor had been in a kitchen where someone was making strawberry jam!

I raced up the stairs, clicking on the lights as I went, and skidded into my room with Vesuvius almost under my feet. Every drawer in my dresser had been pulled out, my closet door stood open, and the box that had been on the shelf was gone. On the floor at my feet was a small, wilted flower with a very short stem, a dainty red rosebud with one curling leaf. It was about the size of a boutonniere—perfect for a man's lapel. Yet I was almost certain it was a woman who had collided with me on the landing. Although it had been dark and our encounter brief, I had the distinct impression the prowler was much shorter than I, and the whiff of strawberries lent credence to the theory of a female intruder.

I sat abruptly on the bed, twirling the rosebud in my fingers. It had come, no doubt, from one of Miss Delia Squires's bushes, yet her brother Nevin always wore a flower in his lapel.

I lay back and frowned at the ceiling. Miss Delia had been our burglar. I was almost sure she had bribed Vesuvius with the ham bone after phoning first to see if anyone was at home. Then she had walked boldly inside and up the stairs to look for Amanda's trinkets. If any of the neighbors had seen her, they wouldn't have thought twice about her dropping by, probably to return a casserole dish or to bring some flowers from her garden.

And her mission hadn't taken very long. I was probably already out of the shower when she came, or else the sound of running water would have frightened her away.

But why on earth had she done it, and what had she been looking for? The stolen box contained not only Amanda's locket and lamb, but the card from Nevin as well.

Nevin. I looked at the rosebud again. Miss Delia never wore a flower. Nevin Squires did. Had she dropped the rose deliberately to incriminate her brother?

I squelched an impulse to phone Austin. He became upset when I cast suspicion on his uncle; what would he do if I told him I thought his sweet maiden aunt had broken into our house? Besides, Austin knew I had the card from Nevin and Amanda's sad possessions. How did I know he wasn't behind the theft?

Vesuvius jumped as I suddenly sat up and smacked my fist into a pillow. If Miss Delia Squires wanted to play cops and robbers, that was fine with me. Tomorrow I would drive out to Willowbend and question her face to face. Austin Leatherwood wouldn't have to know a thing about it!

I wasn't counting on his calling me the next morning just as I was about to leave to confront his aunt.

"Laura, have you learned any more about this Lee person you've been asking about?" he asked.

"Just that she might have been Amanda's sister," I said.

"I think this whole thing hinges on Amanda," he said. "Once we find out what happened to her, we might learn who's behind all this."

I agreed.

"And if there was a sister named Lee, she'd be the one to tell us," he continued.

"But the Scoggins family moved away years ago," I said. "How are we going to find her?"

"I think we should try Grandfather again, or Aunt Delia; they seem to remember the family best, and Amanda was about my aunt's age."

Could Austin hear my quick intake of breath? With one finger I traced the edge of the battered phone table in the hall. The bottom rung had been scuffed by Laney's shoes during her lengthy conversations with this same man only a few years ago. Why did that seem like ancient history?

"Well, what do you think?" Austin paused. "Laura, are you there?"

"Yes, but I don't know, Austin. If you want my opinion, for what it's worth, I don't think it's such a good idea. Your grandfather said—"

"I know very well what His Grace said," he snapped. "Maybe we'll catch him in a better mood; after all, he's due for one sometime this year. We could get lucky."

"Look, I'm not arguing with your grandfather," I began. "Besides, I'd rather not—"

Austin spoke as though he were dictating instructions. "I have a business appointment at eleven," he said, "but I should be through by half-past noon. Be ready." I was listening to a dial tone.

I STARED OUT the window as we drove to Willowbend, shivering slightly in the air-conditioned car. At least Austin hadn't come for me in his disreputable truck. I forced myself not to fidget as we drove up the now-familiar drive to the ugly yellow house. I was not looking forward to seeing the arrogant old judge, and what in the world was I going to say to Miss Delia? (Nice running into you again?)

Judge Decatur Squires jerked open the door as though he were expecting us; then his face took on an obvious look of chagrin. I don't think he wanted to ask us in, but his upbringing demanded it. As we followed him into the hall, I noticed subtle signs of disarray: wilted roses in a vase, a wrinkled shirt tossed over a chair.

"I'm afraid I don't have much to offer in the way of a decent meal," he said, "but you're welcome to join me in whatever we can find." He marched in front of us into the kitchen. "Your Aunt Delia's not here just now."

He must have noticed my look of dismay at the dishes piled in the sink because he quickly stepped in front of it.

Austin stood silently with his mouth slightly open. "Where is she?" he asked bluntly. He acted as though someone had told him they had moved the whole state of South Carolina to the West Coast.

The judge opened the refrigerator. "There's some left-over green beans," he mused, "plenty of ham ..."

"Grandfather, where is she?" Austin asked again with an edge to his voice.

The old man turned, a covered platter in his hand. "How the hell should I know? She took off, vamoosed, been gone since yesterday!"

"She didn't say where she was going?" Austin looked into the pantry as if he expected to see his aunt sitting primly on the shelf with the watermelon rind preserves and chow-chow. I managed to sneak a look over his shoulder. A whole shelf was filled with pint jars of strawberry preserves.

"Looks like she's been busy," I said, trying to examine the date on a label without seeming obvious.

"Cooked all day yesterday, put up those preserves, and then left." He slammed the platter onto the table. "Didn't even have the courtesy to tell me she was leaving!"

"You don't know where she is?" Austin's face was white.

"Nevin said she called him yesterday afternoon at the library and said she was going out of town for a while." He stared numbly at the platter on the table. I noticed a food stain on his tie. "She didn't say where."

I almost felt sorry for him. "I'm sure she'll be back soon," I said. But I didn't really believe it. I wouldn't blame Delia Squires if she never came back to Willowbend, but I wish she hadn't disappeared before we had had a chance to talk.

"Where do you suppose your aunt is?" I asked Austin as we walked to the car. We had left his grandfather having a lonely meal of ham, cold cornbread, and buttermilk. I was getting kind of hungry myself.

He shook his head. "I can't imagine, but Mother might know. Aunt Delia was always her favorite." He frowned as we started back to town. "Well, we certainly didn't learn any more about Amanda's family, did we? I was so stunned over Aunt Delia's not being there, I didn't even think to ask."

"I don't think it would have done any good," I said. Then I grabbed his arm as we passed a familiar side road. "Wait! Turn around, Austin. We forgot about Miss Annie."

"Miss Annie? What about her?"

"Miss Annie Potts! She used to teach the Scogginses, and she just might know where we could get in touch with one of Amanda's brothers or sisters. She lives back there on that street we just passed."

"This won't take long, will it?" Austin asked as we turned into the two-lane asphalt road. "I really need to get back to town."

"Why? What's the rush?" I asked. "You didn't seem to be in any hurry before."

We stopped in the shade of a pecan tree beside Miss Annie's white frame cottage. "That was before I knew about Aunt Delia," he said, switching off the ignition. "She's never gone off like this before, Laura. Something's not right."

TWENTY-TWO

WE WERE JUST IN TIME for pie, homemade peach pie warm from baking, with a generous mound of vanilla ice cream melting over the top. I could almost feel my waistband getting snugger.

"Surely you're not asking me to remember all that lot," our hostess said, dabbing her lips with a napkin. "Some of those Scogginses were half grown when they came here. Amanda was the youngest."

"My uncle said he thought there was a girl named Lee," Austin said.

Miss Annie Potts stacked our empty plates in the sink and leaned against the kitchen counter. "There probably was—don't remember; I only taught the younger ones."

I smiled as Austin started at her voice. I had forgotten to warn him of our former teacher's deafness.

"Now, Ben Ray still lives around here somewhere," she continued. "Works over yonder at the lumberyard, or he used to. I see him every now and then."

"Ben Ray?" I glanced at Austin, who shrugged.

"Ben Ray Scoggins, Amanda's brother," Miss Annie explained. "He was a year or two older than she was, but she could read circles around him." She swung at a fly with a rolled-up newspaper. "Doubt if he ever made it past the eighth grade."

"Ben Ray." Austin sat up straighter. "Is he tall and kind of stoop-shouldered with gray hair? Sort of thin?"

Miss Annie nodded. "You could thread him through a needle."

"I've seen him; I think he still works there." Austin stood quickly. "If we hurry, Laura, maybe we can see him before I have to get back to the office."

Miss Annie followed us to the door. "Come back when you can stay longer," she said. "Maybe next time I'll have a painting for you."

Austin laughed when I told him about the painting Miss Annie had sent Aunt Nell, but he didn't have much to say as we drove back to town. I think he was still worried about his aunt's sudden disappearance. I couldn't help but wonder what Austin's dignified family would say if they knew Delia Squires had spent a part of the night before lurking on our stairs!

We found Ben Ray Scoggins loading two-by-fours onto a truck at the back of the lumberyard. He seemed glad for an excuse for a break and followed us into the relative shade of a lean-to, mopping his face with a soiled handkerchief.

"Miss Annie Potts suggested we talk with you," Austin explained, and the man's puzzled expression broke into a smile. "We're trying to find out what happened to your sister Amanda, how she died."

Ben Ray nodded solemnly. "She drowned...in the river there."

"Do you remember how it happened, Mr. Scoggins?" I asked. "Were you there at the time?"

Slowly he stuffed the handkerchief into the pocket of his overalls. "Well, that were a long time ago. I don't remember too much about it. Besides, we'd already left by then," he said. "But Amanda, she stayed behind."

"Left for where?" Austin asked. "What do you mean, you left?"

"We was living down near Spartanburg then," Ben Ray said. "Mama and Daddy was picking peaches that summer." He rubbed a grimy arm across his forehead and grinned. "We all was."

"But Amanda stayed behind," Austin persisted. "Why?"

The older man frowned. In spite of his work in the sun, his thin face was pale beneath a stubble of beard. "Mama never said why. I always reckoned she was visiting; she and that other little girl, the little girl that lived there, they was good friends."

"What little girl?" I asked. "Do you mean Miss Delia? Delia Squires?"

He smiled, showing yellowed teeth. I couldn't believe this man was Amanda's brother. "Yeah, her. They was in the same grade together."

Looking over his shoulder, Ben Ray pulled a pack of cigarettes from his front pocket and cupped his hands to light one, although there was no breeze. "I always felt real bad about Amanda. Her and me was the youngest, you know. When Goldie Lee told me she'd drowned, I got plumb sick to my stomach."

"Goldie Lee?" I gulped air. The smell of raw sawdust burned my nostrils.

"My sister Goldie Lee. Amanda was like her baby doll. She drug her around everywhere, and when she found out how Amanda had died, she just sat around and cried. Wouldn't eat, wouldn't work, nothing." The smoke from his cigarette hung in the sluggish air. "That was the summer she run away, run off and got married." He flicked the cigarette to the floor and ground it under his foot. "She warn't but seventeen."

"Mr. Scoggins, where is Goldie Lee now?" I asked. "Do you know where we can get in touch with her?"

Ben Ray stuck his thumbs in his overalls pockets and reared back with pride. "Sure do. Got her own shop,

Goldie does, over in Fayetteville. She always did have a mind for business." He pulled a dingy card from his wallet and passed it to me. "Goldie's Garden of Gifts" was printed on it in flowing script. I copied the address and phone number while pouring out my thanks. I could hardly wait for the man to leave the shed so I could check and see if that cigarette was really out under all the sawdust.

"He can't be Amanda's brother," I said to Austin as we drove to Aunt Nell's. "I don't believe she was related to any of them."

He smiled. "I don't know. Goldie Lee seems to have done all right for herself. Besides, how do you know what Amanda was like? You've never seen her, not really. She might have been a female Ben Ray if she had lived."

"Never," I said. "Your Aunt Delia said she always wore a blue ribbon in her hair."

"So?"

"Austin Leatherwood, you're an insensitive clod! A little girl who always wore a blue ribbon could never turn out like Ben Ray Scoggins."

He glanced at the clock on his dashboard. "Look, I have to get back, but I do want to be there when you talk with Goldie Lee. Can it wait until tomorrow?"

"No way," I said. "Besides, it should only take a few minutes. Come on in, there's an extension upstairs. We'll both talk to her."

Austin looked at my aunt's house, then back to me. "I can't, Laura, not yet. I can't go in there."

"What do you mean?"

"I just feel ... well, peculiar. And your aunt acts as though I've done something wrong. I think she believes I might have had something to do with Laney's death."

I didn't know what to say. I couldn't argue with him because I knew what he said was true. I took his hand in mine and briefly laced our fingers together. Would he ever get over Laney's death? Would I? "Things are rough for Aunt Nell right now; just give her a little time."

He lifted my hand, still locked in his, and kissed it. *Kissed it.* I practically floated out of the car and up the steps. I felt sixteen again. Was Laney somewhere watching? Could she see? Did she care?

"I'll call later," Austin had said as he left. Of course he wanted to know the results of my call to Fayetteville, but at least he would be in touch. I could look forward to hearing his voice again. And what a warm, wonderful voice it was. I wondered why I had never noticed that before. Maybe I had.

My aunt stirred cake batter at the kitchen table while watching Will playing with a toy car on the back porch. A sleeping Vesuvius provided the mountain range for the miniature travelers inside. He didn't seem to mind.

Aunt Nell smiled. "His father's coming for supper," she whispered. "Do you think he'll like boiled shrimp and garlic bread?"

I hugged her. "Doesn't everybody?"

"I've made a salad and thrown together this cake," she said, "if you'll just pick up the shrimp. They're holding some for us at the market." My aunt caught my chin in her hand and rubbed her finger across my cheek. "You've dirt all over you, Laura. Where in the world have you been?"

For a minute I thought she was going to spit on a hankie and use it to wash my face as she had when Laney and I were little. I told her about our conversation with Ben Ray Scoggins, being careful not to mention Austin any more than necessary. "And there was a sister named

Goldie Lee, who could have given Amanda that locket,"
I said. "I'm going to call her right now."

She put her head on one side and frowned at me. "I
think you ought to wear that yellow sundress tonight,
Laura. It brings out the highlights in your hair."

I pretended not to hear her as I went outside to play with
the only two uncomplicated males in my world. They ate,
they slept, they played. What else mattered? If only my life
could be that simple. My well-meaning aunt was trying to
cook up a romance between me and Will's father. But she
was too late, and I didn't know how to tell her.

TWENTY-THREE

"YES, this is Goldie Lee Ryan." The voice was polished and businesslike, yet it still retained some of its rural flatness. I wondered what she looked like, this aging sister of Amanda's. She would have to have a certain amount of ruggedness about her to have overcome her squalid beginnings; yet she would be tender, too, tender enough to have grieved over the death of a child who wore a blue ribbon in her hair.

I started with the locket. "It had the name Lee inside," I said, "and your brother said you were close to Amanda. I thought you might have given it to her."

"Can you wait just a minute?" she asked, and I heard the sound of a door closing. This was to be a private conversation.

She sounded a little breathless as she picked up the phone. "About that locket. Amanda always had it, I think. I don't know where it came from." She sighed. "Wasn't me. I tried to take care of her, though, keep her clean. I like to died when we had to leave her behind, and then they told me she'd died! Drowned in that dirty river!"

There was silence on the line. Was the woman crying? "Jud and me—that's my husband—well, we had three of our own, but I never loved a one of them more than Amanda. I can see her now, pretty little thing, and so smart, too!"

"Mrs. Ryan, do you remember when Amanda was born?" I asked. "I know it's a lot to ask; after all, you were only a child yourself."

"Honey, I knew a lot at that age, earlier than that. I was eight when Amanda came, and I remember helping when Ben Ray was born, but not Amanda. One day Mama said we were gonna have a baby sister, and the next day she was there. Just like that!"

"Your mother knew the baby was going to be a girl?"

"I didn't think much about it then, but yes, I think she did. I've wondered since if Amanda really belonged to us. She sure didn't fit in with the rest."

"Ben Ray said she was left behind," I said. "The summer she died, the rest of you went to pick peaches, but Amanda stayed here. Why?"

"Have you ever seen those places where migrant workers stay?" she asked. "There wasn't room for her, and she was too young to do much work. Mama said we'd get her later, at the end of the summer. But then she died.... I named my oldest girl after her; she teaches up in Raleigh now. Smart, like her aunt was."

I smiled. "I know Amanda would be proud," I said. Tears stung my eyes as I hung up the phone. I thought I knew who had tied the blue ribbons in Amanda's hair, and if I ever found the locket again, I would see that it got to the person who'd loved her the most.

Austin had not called by the time I got back from the market with the shrimp, and I knew he was probably having to do twice the work to make up for the time he had spent with me tracking the mysterious Lee.

To humor my aunt, I wore the yellow sundress when I went downstairs to set the table for dinner, and she smiled approvingly.

"Now, that's more like it. You look pretty, Laura. Why don't you play for us some after supper? I think Sidney would enjoy it, and I know I would." She tried to behave as if this were a sudden inspiration, but she was not a very good actress, and I knew a plot when I heard one: the dinner, the music, the cozy family scene. I was relieved when the phone rang and ran upstairs to answer it.

"Goldie Lee didn't give Amanda the locket," I told Austin. "She doesn't know where it came from." I wound the telephone cord around my finger. "Look, we need to talk. Can you come by later?"

He sighed. "I don't think so, Laura. Aunt Delia's still missing, and no one seems to have the vaguest notion where she is. I just came back from Mother's, and she laughed at me! Her own sister is gone, and she acts like she doesn't even care!"

I felt like laughing, too. "My goodness, Austin, your aunt's a middle-aged woman. It's time she got away from home. Besides, she called your Uncle Nevin, didn't she?"

"Yeah, well, that's what Grandfather said."

The awful thought crossed my mind that either Austin didn't trust his own family, or they didn't trust him.

"I'll come by later if I can, but don't count on it," he said. "There's something I have to do." Then almost as if it were an afterthought, he asked, "Is this something urgent, Laura, or can it wait until tomorrow?"

"I guess it can wait; it's just a feeling." How did you explain a feeling? I paused, trying to force my awareness into words. Downstairs, I heard my aunt greeting Sidney Marshall at the door.

"What kind of feeling?" Maybe I was being unusually sensitive, but Austin sounded as if he were only asking to be polite. I guess he had troubles enough of his own.

"Like everything is flying in bits and pieces, all in one direction, and I'm right there in the middle, Austin. So are you!"

I stopped. I felt as if nothing I said had made a lick of sense. "It's like we're all being drawn by a magnet," I added, "and Laney is the force behind it: Laney and Amanda, and whatever happened on Crybaby Bridge."

Austin started to say something, but I cut him off. Aunt Nell was calling me to come downstairs, and as far as I was concerned, the conversation was over. Besides, it was nothing that couldn't wait another day.

Or so I thought. And I did temporarily forget my problems during the meal. Sidney Marshall was a relaxing dinner guest with a droll sense of humor, and I could see why he had appealed to Laney. Since the young vet and my Aunt Nell had declared a truce, they seemed to get along well together, teasing one another and bragging about Will. The poor child was going to have an ego as big as the moon.

I enjoyed playing the piano after dinner. Not only was it restful, but it didn't require me to talk, and for a short, happy time I forgot about Laney. In fact, I would have enjoyed the entire evening if I hadn't known I was being set up for marriage. I wondered if Sidney knew it, too. Maybe he didn't care.

When Aunt Nell left the two of us on the porch in the dark on the pretext of checking Will, Sidney asked my help in finding an apartment. He had accepted Doc Ratteree's offer in order to be near Will, and his present quarters were too small.

I knew of a vine-covered cottage for three with a picket fence around it, but it was only in my aunt's mind. Of course I didn't tell him that, but I promised to help him look for a place where Will could visit on weekends. When Sidney left, he took my hand and kissed me lightly on the cheek. "Call you later," he said.

I sat alone in the porch swing after my aunt went to bed. Was I merely collecting my cousin's cast-offs? Cast off or not, I would have to discourage Sidney Marshall. He was an attractive man and a caring father, and it would certainly tie things up in a neat little package if the two of us married, but I could only love one man at a time.

With my luck, it was probably the wrong one.

TWENTY-FOUR

I WAS A FOOL to come here. A light summer rain fell, and the moon was shrouded with hovering clouds; yet the outline of the bridge towered dark and imposing against the somber sky.

With Vesuvius curled asleep in the back of Laney's Volkswagen, I pulled off the narrow road into the tree-bordered clearing overlooking the river. High school couples came here to make out and drink beer, but there was no one parked here tonight. No one but me and a heart full of troubled memories.

Both my aunt and Will were sleeping soundly after an exhausting day, but I knew it was useless to try. Too many unanswered questions tumbled about in my mind. Had Delia Squires really gotten in touch with her brother? Why did she suddenly go away, and where? I was almost sure there was a connection between Austin's meek aunt and Amanda's death. Now, had something happened to Delia as well?

And who had sent the note in Laney's handwriting? Goldie Lee Ryan might want to revive an interest, possibly an investigation, into the way Amanda died, but how could she be familiar with Laney's handwriting? Besides, she didn't live anywhere near Bishopville.

The old bridge rattled ominously as a lone car drove across, then rounded the curve and disappeared. Few people came this way, especially this late at night. I switched on the dome light to look at my watch. It was just after ten, not quite as late as I thought. Sidney had left around nine, explaining that he had an early day tomorrow, and I had persuaded Aunt Nell to retire early and leave the cleaning up to me. I had no intention of driving alone (except for a cowardly dog) out to Crybaby Bridge on a damp, murky night. I hated this place, despised it. But it had pulled at me all day, had been compelling me to return the whole time I had been back in Redpath. And it was all because of Laney.

Large drops of rain spattered on my windshield, but it had been crisp and clear the night we came here after the football game our junior year in high school. After a series of losses, the Warriors had finally won, and we exulted in our victory, at least twenty-five of us, packed into three cars and eager to celebrate....

SOMEBODY'S ELBOW jabbed into my side, and I shifted on the bony lap that held me. I was glad when we stopped and the car doors opened at once, releasing us to the cold November air.

"Hey, it's freezing! Let's build a bonfire!" It was Laney, tumbling from the car behind us, jumping up and down to keep warm. She wore jeans and a bulky sweater; no amount of pleading on Aunt Nell's part could convince her to wear a wrap.

Our breath made smoke signals in the air in spite of the bonfire's crackling boasts of warmth, and I stamped my numbing feet for feeling.

"Who's got the beer?" someone called.

"Over here! Drink it fast before it freezes!"

A gloved hand thrust a cold can at me. I didn't want it. I had never tasted beer before. Across the bonfire Laney tried to teach the cancan to Austin and Bo Benedict, the cute new quarterback with Paul Newman eyes. Her cheeks were flushed; her bright hair bounced.

"Let's all do a line dance across the bridge!" My cousin giggled, an arm around each boy's waist. I knew she wasn't drinking. She didn't have to. She was high on being sixteen and beautiful. "Come on!" she shouted. "Maybe we'll hear the baby cry."

I shivered. I couldn't go out on that bridge at night, not even with a crowd of rowdy friends. The laughing, shouting line wound out of sight, leaving me behind, and thundered across the planks until it sounded as if the whole outdated structure would shudder and collapse, dumping them all in the icy river.

I started to call out to them, to run after them; I didn't like being left alone. But I wasn't alone.

"Taste it, you'll like it." Greg Arnold was a year older than I was and had been offered a scholarship to play football at Carolina. He was tall, he was handsome, and he had an arm around me. "Just take a big gulp," he said in my ear.

I did. It was awful! I couldn't spit it out, not right in front of Greg. I made some sort of weird sound as I swallowed.

"There, what'd I tell you?" He gave my shoulder a squeeze. "Bottoms up!"

I drank over half the can before I began to feel sick. Greg nuzzled my neck; he smelled sour, and his hand roamed under my jacket. I tried to shove him away.

"Laura! Some of us are going back to town for hamburgers. Want a ride?" Austin called to me as he herded a group into his car. It was not the car I had come in, but I didn't care.

"Yes, wait!" I called. I couldn't get there fast enough, couldn't put enough distance between Greg and me. I looked around for Laney, but she was nowhere in sight. And neither was Bo Benedict. . . .

THE RAIN was slacking now, and Laney's small car was close and muggy. I needed to breathe, to stretch. "Come on, Vesuvius. Wake up, boy!" I prodded my sleeping companion in the back seat, and he looked at me with one eye. Was I crazy? Couldn't I see it was wet out there, and late besides? Time for sleep. And Vesuvius did.

"Fair-weather friend!" I left him there and walked to the edge of the clearing. The place hadn't changed since the last time I had come here with Buddy Callahan the summer after we graduated from high school. We doubledated with Laney and Austin, and the two of them had argued most of the evening. We would soon be leaving for college, and Laney wanted to date other people. Austin didn't. They left Buddy and me in the car while they walked back and forth across the bridge, their angry voices cutting through the night.

I understood what Laney was trying to do, but she was going about it wrong. There must be a gentler way to let poor Austin down. I hated seeing him hurt. I wanted to go home, to shut out the anger and sadness.

But Buddy had other ideas. He had tried all year to get me to park with him alone, and the situation was ideal. Laney and Austin were embroiled in their own problems; we had the car to ourselves, and I was fair game.

He lunged for me as if I were a football, and he were headed for the end zone. Fortunately he fumbled, and I slipped out of his grasp.

"Hey, cool it, will you, Buddy? They'll be back in a minute!" I tried to make light of the circumstances, but I was a little bit scared. Buddy was a lot bigger than I was, and he was so thick-headed and egotistical, he thought I was merely being coy. Already I had seen him for what he was, coming on to any girl who encouraged him while pretending I was his one and only, and I had made up my mind that this would be our last date. I was tired of fighting. When I was ready for sex, it wouldn't be in the back seat of a car, and it wouldn't be with Buddy Callahan—not if I could help it. I planted my palms in his chest. "Quit it, Buddy! Somebody might see us."

"Who cares? Laura, I need you. Be nice to me, please?" He snatched me to him, tried to force his tongue into my mouth. I clenched my teeth and came down on his instep with the heel of my shoe.

"Don't do something you'll regret, Buddy," I reminded him. "Think of all those freshman girls you'll be meeting in a few weeks. Maybe some of them will be ready for this, I'm not!"

To my surprise, he smiled. "Heck, Laura, you can't blame me for trying." He shrugged and kissed my cheek, and I relaxed for the first time that night. Then suddenly, we heard Austin shout, "No! Laney, no! Come down!"

Fear raced through me like a current. My whole body ran on its power. Buddy and I scrambled to the bridge and found Laney climbing high on the framework while Austin paced beneath, pleading.

"It's okay, Laney, I promise. Just come down. Please don't go any higher! I didn't mean what I said." Austin turned to me. "Laura, talk to her, see what you can do."

I looked up at the silhouette of my cousin. In the darkness she seemed to be balancing on nothing. Below I heard the sweep of the river. Someone cried...a baby?

"This isn't funny, Laney. Don't do this, please!" I begged. She held something over the water, something on a chain. Austin's class ring? Car keys? They jangled.

"No! No! Laney, give me the keys! Don't, please don't..."

FOOTSTEPS SOUNDED behind me, running footsteps, pounding across the bridge. "Laura, Laura! It's all right. Oh God, what are you doing here? What are you trying to prove?" Austin's arms went around me, drawing me close, holding me. I clung to him and cried. A steady drizzle of rain began as we stood there locked together on Crybaby Bridge. How on earth did I get there? What was happening to me?

"Here, you're getting soaking wet." Austin walked me to his car, which was parked on the other end of the bridge, and got in beside me.

"How did you know where to find me?" I asked.

"I had an idea you'd come here after what you said earlier." Austin drove over the narrow bridge and parked off the road beside my car. Vesuvius was an inert shadow in the back. "When I drove by your aunt's earlier and saw the Volkswagen wasn't there, I knew you must be here." Austin took me firmly by the shoulders. "Why, Laura? What in the world was going on out there on that bridge?"

I shivered, and he wrapped a sweater around my shoulders. "Remember the night Laney gave you back your ring? Remember how she climbed on the bridge, Austin? Well, it all came back to me; it was almost like it was happening all over again." I frowned. "I don't even remember walking onto the bridge. All of a sudden I was there, and then you were there beside me."

"You scared the hell out of me, Laura." Austin shook his head as if he could throw off his fear. "Don't ever do that again."

I wrapped myself in the sweater. It smelled kind of musty but nice. "I'm sorry, but believe me, I didn't do it on purpose. It just sort of happened."

"I know that, Laura." He spoke softly, somewhere near my ear.

"But why did she do that, Austin? The night you and Laney broke up, what made her climb up on that bridge? I don't think she realized how she scared us when she did things like that."

"Of course she did!" Austin's jarring comment shocked me. "That's exactly why she did them, Laura. Laney liked attention, but most of all she liked to win, to be on top of a situation. That night I accused her of using people, men especially, and she was making me suffer for it."

"But everybody does that!" I said. "We all use people. We might not realize it, but it's true."

"Yes, but Laney played a game. She collected men, like a kid collects dolls or baseball cards and then outgrows them."

"And that's why she climbed on the bridge?"

Austin nodded. "She didn't accept criticism very well. I knew Laney wasn't going to throw herself in the river, but I was afraid she might fall." He found my hand in the darkness. "She threatened to toss in my class ring, too, remember? I don't know why she didn't, but after that little episode, I didn't argue anymore about getting back together. I loved Laney, and I hurt when all that ended, but I knew she was wrong for me. I think she knew it, too."

"But I thought—"

"You thought I was carrying a torch for your cousin all this time; a lot of people did." He smiled. "Remember that winter when we were about twelve and had that big snow? Everybody scrounged up trays or cardboard boxes or whatever they could find to slide on, and we all went over to Echo Hill?" He played with the cuff on my sweater sleeve, turning it up, then down. "Loving Laney was a little like that," he said, "fast and exciting, unpredictable, but eventually that gets tiresome. There comes a time when you want to go home and put on dry socks and have a nice hot bowl of chicken noodle soup.

"Maybe it's because I never married, never settled down," he went on. "And then when Laney came home to work with Doc Ratteree, everybody said, 'Oh, how sweet—they're together again!'" Austin laughed. "I think for a while Laney thought there was a chance we could take up where we'd left off in high school. She wanted a father for Will, and I was her first choice."

"Will has a father," I said.

"I know. Sidney Marshall. Laney finally told me."

"Then why would she want to marry you?" Warm again, I threw off the sweater.

He feigned a hurt expression. "Doesn't every woman?"

"Silly. You know what I mean."

"Laney didn't love Sid, and she knew he had come back and was looking for her," Austin explained. "I think she was afraid he would try to take Will away. If she was safely married to me, she could claim Will was mine, and Sidney wouldn't stand a chance." He looked at me then, and although his mouth was smiling, his eyes were not. His face was so near, I could feel his breath, and he smelled brisk and clean, like strong soap. "Laney told me I was the closest she ever came to falling in love," he admitted.

"Close isn't enough," I said.

"No," he said, kissing me, "it isn't."

TWENTY-FIVE

AUSTIN AND I spent the weekend trying to help Sidney Marshall find a place to live. I think Aunt Nell believed that Sid and I were becoming a romantic twosome and that Austin was the unlucky odd-man-out.

Sidney, however, was not as naive, and he was in our company only a short time before he caught on. "Why does it seem that I'm always losing out to you?" he said to Austin with a good-natured shrug. At least I hoped it was a good-natured shrug. I liked Sidney; his love for Will was obvious. But I just wasn't sure of him yet. Too many things had been happening that had no explanation for me to accept anyone at face value.

By Sunday afternoon we had had no luck in finding Sid an apartment and no word from Austin's Aunt Delia. Although I had checked the mail faithfully, I didn't receive any more messages in Laney's hasty scrawl. It seemed as if we had come to a standstill in our efforts to find out what had happened to Amanda.

I didn't have any rational explanation for my strange experience on Crybaby Bridge. Laney had no intention of jumping from the bridge that summer night, Austin had pointed out. But eventually she had jumped, or had fallen, or maybe she was thrown, and none of us had been there to stop her.

And why did I see car keys in her hand when Austin said she dangled his class ring over the water? Even with my eyes closed, I saw those keys, heard them jangling in my dreams.

Sunday night Sid telephoned to say he had rented a small house within walking distance of Aunt Nell's, and that as soon as he moved in, we were all invited for barbecue.

"Sounds great," Austin said when I told him. "Poor guy, he was another victim of Laney's great love-in experience. I hope he'll find a nice girl who makes rice pudding and wears her hair in a bun."

I made a face. "Rice pudding! And I suppose he'll have to settle for plain comforts like chicken noodle soup and dry socks. How boring!"

He frowned. "What are you talking about?"

"That's what you implied. Laney was like a thrilling zip through the snow, and I'm an ordinary bowl of soup—canned soup at that!"

"I said no such thing." Austin tried to kiss me, but he was laughing too hard. "But a combination would be nice: an exhilarating sleigh ride topped off with a dish of oyster stew." He winked. "Good for your sex life."

I laughed and snuggled closer on the sofa. The two of us were sitting with Will while Aunt Nell went to a wedding. I was afraid it was going to give her notions; she seemed to have weddings on her mind.

I sat up suddenly. "My car's supposed to be ready by late tomorrow," I said. "Could you drive me by Sam's to pick it up?"

He groaned. "I'll be gone most of the afternoon. I doubt if I'll be back in time. Can't your aunt drop you off?"

"Sure, I just thought—Austin, you're not going out looking for your Aunt Delia, are you? Why all the mystery?"

"Of course not! I wouldn't even know where to look; besides, Mother doesn't seem the least concerned. I'm sure she knows where she is." He smiled as if he were sizing me up. "Oh, I suppose it's okay to tell you, but I haven't said anything to my folks yet. I'm taking a few refresher courses at the University extension this summer. I've been accepted into law school next term."

"Austin, that's wonderful! But why all the secrecy?"

"This is what I wanted all along," he admitted, "but Dad needed me to help with the business. His health wasn't good when I got out of college, so I decided to stick around for a while. Now Dad's stronger and so's the firm. I'll still be able to pop in now and then if they need me, but I think I've stuck around long enough." He gripped my fingers tightly. "I was going to tell them tomorrow night. Come with me for courage?"

I laughed. "Fight your own battles! Besides, your mother doesn't like me. She might pass out from shock if you drag me over there."

"What makes you say that?"

"I'm Laney's cousin, aren't I? Now don't try to tell me your mother was keen on that match!" I held his face so he couldn't avoid my eyes. "Austin Leatherwood, everybody in town knows your mother wants you to marry Blakely Floyd."

He squirmed out of my grasp. "Then everybody in town will be disappointed, including my mother—if that's what she really wants."

Now it was my turn to be interrogated. He held my chin firmly, "Now, you tell me honestly, Laura Graham. If you had a son, would you want him to marry someone like Laney?"

"Laney had a lot of good qualities," I said defensively.

"That's not what I asked."

I tried to look down, up, to duck away.

"Answer me," he said.

I sighed. "I guess not."

Austin kissed my chin. "The defense rests. Now, if you'll come by the folks' for a drink tomorrow night, I'll invite you over to my place afterward for dinner."

"Who's cooking?"

"You are, of course," he teased. "No, I guess I'll have to be fair. We both will. What's your specialty?"

I giggled. "Chicken noodle soup. I'm not that great a cook."

"Neither am I," he said. "I know—bring that rich chocolate thing you used to make. You served it warm with ice cream . . . ummm . . . what was it?"

"Fudge pie? There's not much to it, but I'll bring it if you like, for what it's worth."

"Stop saying that!"

I jumped back, frightened. His words stunned me. I wasn't used to having someone bark in my face.

"Do you realize how often you say that?" Austin's voice was even now, but his face was red, and he seemed to be having trouble keeping his emotions in check. "Quit putting yourself down, Laura. Have a little confidence in yourself."

I felt my lip start to quiver. "I don't—"

"Yes, you do; you always have." He pulled me toward him. "You gave up your music because you thought you weren't good enough, didn't you?"

"Well, yes, but I really don't think I could've made it, Austin. That's a tough field." I looked up at him. "What is this, anyway? If I wanted a relationship with a psychologist, I'd have stuck with the man I had!"

"I just don't like your being so hard on yourself. You don't have to compete with Laney anymore."

I moved away from him. Was he being deliberately cruel? But there was some truth in what he had said. I remembered the times my aunt had asked me to play when

Laney had "better" things to do. "Oh, forget that old piano, Laura. You can do that anytime!" It wasn't important... I wasn't important....

"What a nasty thing to say!" I glared at him through tears.

He didn't try to touch me. "Maybe so, but it's true. I want you to see yourself the way I see you: you're pretty, you're intelligent, and I've always thought you were the best dancer in our class." He grinned. "Did you know that I was going to ask you to the prom our junior year in high—"

I whirled away. "Stop! I don't want to hear it."

"Why not?" He followed me across the room, stuck to me like wallpaper. "What's the matter with you, Laura? I *was* going to ask you to the prom, but Laney—"

"Please, Austin, don't! I'd rather not talk about it." My head throbbed so, it hurt to move; my vision blurred.

He eased me onto the sofa; his touch was light on my arm. "Laura, look, I'm sorry. What's wrong? Can I get you something?"

"There's a prescription in my handbag." I closed my eyes and heard him scrambling frantically for the bottle. I swallowed the pill gratefully. I had been having these headaches lately, but it had been a long time since I had had an attack this bad. I was afraid to move or to open my eyes, afraid I would be deathly sick.

"Laura, you're scaring me," Austin said. "Do you want me to call a doctor?"

I tried to smile. "No, I'll be fine, I promise, but I'd rather be alone right now. I'll just rest down here in the dark."

"Are you sure? What if Will awakes?"

"He won't. Besides, Aunt Nell's due any minute." I felt the pill taking effect and sank into the pillow. "Really, it's okay. I'll see you tomorrow. And thanks," I added as he touched my forehead with a kiss.

Austin turned out the lamp as he left. "I'll call you in the morning," he promised.

AND HE DID. "You sound like a different person," he said. "You must be feeling better."

"Like a new woman," I agreed. Once the strange headache left, it was as if I had never been sick at all. I had just eaten an enormous breakfast of assorted fattening goodies and was flipping through my aunt's cookbooks to make more.

"I think I've found that recipe you like," I told him, marking the page with my finger. "I'll stir us up a batch of calories for dessert tonight."

"Great. I'll make a salad, and we'll throw some steaks on the grill. And Laura...my parents are expecting you for drinks around six. I'll meet you there."

"But Austin, I—" I must have stood there for a full minute holding the receiver in my hand after Austin had hung up laughing.

"What are you frowning so about?" My aunt came in from the backyard, where she had been filling Will's wading pool, and a good share of the water was on the front of her dress.

I told her about my invitation for cocktails as we watched my little cousin splashing about.

"I've always kind of admired Daisy Squires—uh, Leatherwood," she said. "A lot of people don't; she's blunt, you know."

"No kidding!" I grinned. "But I thought you couldn't stand her. She made it obvious she didn't like Laney, and you've always made fun of her name."

"Well, she is a little too direct at times, and I'll admit we've had our differences. But when Laney died, she came right over." My aunt absently twirled her glasses in one hand. "And I don't suppose there's much she can do about her name. Just try to keep things in perspective, Laura. With Daisy you always know where you stand."

Was that good or bad? I considered this later that day as I drove to the Leatherwoods' elegant, columned home and parked next to the carpetlike lawn where no weed dared show its unpedigreed face. My compact car seemed enormous after driving Laney's even smaller Volkswagen, but it rode much smoother now and looked almost new with its fresh coat of paint. I gave the fender a fond pat as I walked past.

Austin, his parents, and two rambunctious cocker spaniels met me at the door. I apologized for being a few minutes late. "I had to pick up my car from Sam's," I explained. "Doesn't it look nice with its new paint job?"

Daisy smiled and nodded along with the others, then focused on my car with a fixed stare. "Same color?" she asked finally.

"Yes, I've sort of gotten used to that shade of blue." I glanced over my shining set of wheels. Had Sam missed a spot?

"Well, come on now, let's have a drink, celebrate Austin's good news," his father said. "His grandfather will be mighty proud to have another lawyer in the family."

I waded through the dogs to a large, wicker-filled sun room, where I was seated on a chintz-covered sofa and given a cool drink. Daisy Leatherwood passed a tray of stuffed mushrooms and vegetables with dip, urging everyone to have more. A cordial hostess, she sat beside me with the honey-colored cockers at her feet and asked about

Aunt Nell and Will, but she had a distracted look about her, as if she was preoccupied with something.

Austin's father, I believe, had had a drink or two before we came and was reminiscing in a mellow, reflective mood about his early real estate days when his wife cut him off in midsentence.

"Now I remember!" She glanced at me sharply. "I knew I'd seen your car before. You were here the night your cousin died. I saw that same car in her driveway."

My face grew hot; my throat tightened. Was the woman crazy? "No, you must be mistaken," I said. "I was in Atlanta that night." I looked to Austin for help. "Don't you remember? I called Aunt Nell from there when Laney didn't answer her phone."

But Daisy Leatherwood shook her head. "I know I saw it there," she insisted. "I passed her place on my way to Willowbend right before dark, and I wondered whose car it was. Later, when we heard what had happened, I went over to see if I could help, and it wasn't there anymore."

"That's enough, Mother." Austin came and stood behind me, his hand on my shoulder. "Maybe you did see a blue car, but it wasn't Laura's. She couldn't be in two places at once. You must be confused."

"That's just what puzzles me." His mother stared at me as if I were in a museum showcase. "I'm not confused, and I have a very good memory. It *was* Laura's car I saw." Her speech slowed, almost as if a battery were running down, and it seemed to come from a long distance away. "Why don't you tell the truth, Laura!" she asked. "You were with Laney that night, weren't you? You saw what happened on Crybaby Bridge!"

TWENTY-SIX

COULD THIS BE HAPPENING to me? Was Austin's mother accusing me of having something to do with Laney's death? My head felt as it it had a thunderstorm inside. How could she say those things? I loved Laney. Didn't I?

I SAW HER FACE close to mine, her wet hair whipping about. She laughed and pushed me away, held the car keys over the blustering river. I grabbed for them, tried to wrench them from her, and slipped on the rain-soaked boards. My cousin shoved me, shoved me hard; I heard the keys land with a clank beside me as my head hit the floor of the bridge.

I SHIVERED in the cold rain; icy water dripped into my eyes. I tried to wipe it away, to get to my feet, but something held me back.

"Lie still, Laura." It was Austin's voice. "Mother, you put too much water on that cloth. You don't have to drown her!"

"Daisy, I'll swear to God, you've gone too far this time!" Austin's father spoke from somewhere close beside me. "When are you going to think before you speak? Look what you've done to this poor girl!"

I opened my eyes. Daisy Leatherwood stooped over me with a dripping cloth in her hand. She opened her mouth, but no words came. Then, with a soft little moan, she smoothed my collar, patted me on the shoulder.

Austin offered a glass of water and one of my headache pills, but I turned away. The pain was better now, and I needed a clear head to think. I had blocked it out long enough, that awful night Laney died. It was time to accept what had happened and learn to live with myself.

I struggled to sit up, and Austin sat beside me. "Laura, I'm sorry this happened." He glanced at his mother. "We all are; I hope you'll forgive—"

I shook my head. "No, don't. It's all right, Austin. It's true." The ache in my chest expanded, making it difficult to breathe, and I struggled to speak. Austin didn't let go my hand, although his eyes held shock and horror.

"You were there?" His voice was a whisper. "Laura, why didn't you tell us? Why did you say you were in Atlanta?"

"Because I didn't remember," I said. "I didn't want to remember!" Gradually bits and pieces of that dreadful night had come back to me: the bottle of Scotch in the kitchen, finding my toothpaste in Laney's bathroom, seeing my cousin's favorite jacket—the one she had worn that night. But I didn't want to accept them. I tried to store them in that dark room in my mind where I had shelved the truth, because the truth was more than I could bear.

"I won't blame you if you don't believe me," I said. "But I honestly didn't remember. I couldn't deal with what happened that night, and so I blocked it out." My hand trembled as I took a sip of water. "I guess I did a pretty good job of it until your mother challenged me, made me face it."

"And what did happen, Laura?" Daisy Leatherwood sank onto the cushion beside me, still clutching the damp cloth. It made a dark, wet splotch on her pale lavender dress.

"I'm still not sure exactly," I said. "Laney was acting strangely that night. I had been to a workshop in Greenville and had originally planned to drive back to Atlanta, but she called me again the night before, begging me to come. And then she told me about the note, the note from Amanda, and I was afraid *not* to come, afraid of what she'd do." I looked briefly at Austin and saw the hurt in his eyes. "I wasn't to tell anyone I was coming; she made me promise," I said.

"My God, she must have planned it!" Austin's father looked sick. "No wonder you blocked it out."

"It was dark when I got to Laney's, and she was alone. She didn't say any more about the note, and neither did I. I thought maybe she'd been teasing—or I hoped she had. Will was spending the night with Aunt Nell, she said, because the next day was Saturday, and she planned to...sleep late." I almost choked on the words.

"She offered me a drink of Scotch, and I should have realized then that something was wrong because Laney never kept alcohol in the house. She had bought it for me, she said, and since I was tired and it had been a long day, I accepted."

Austin frowned. "Did she drink with you?"

"No, of course not, but I know now why she had it on hand: we were going out to eat, and she wanted to drive. She wanted an excuse to stop on Crybaby Bridge, and she knew I'd never come that way." My voice rose to a scream before I knew what I was doing. "She did it on purpose! She tricked me! Did she hate me that much?"

"Hey, you don't have to go on, Laura." Austin held me as I cried. "It's all right, it's over now."

But it wasn't over, and it wasn't all right. I held the cool cloth to my face and closed my eyes. "We went to a fast-food restaurant for hamburgers, one of those new places near the mall. Laney didn't want to go in, so we used the drive-in window and ate in the car, or at least I ate. Laney only ordered coffee, said she'd had a big lunch.''

The remembered smell of the greasy food in the closed car made my stomach lurch. As I talked about that night, I could see again the pale profile of my cousin's face against the darkness, hear again the rain thudding on the car as we shared our last meal.

I had slurped every drop from a chocolate shake and polished off a hamburger with everything on it while Laney sipped her coffee silently. She lit a cigarette and exhaled through a crack in the window. The damp March wind found the opening and chilled us with its frigid blast.

"Can't you wait until we get home?" I asked. "It's freezing in here, and my car will smell like smoke for days. Besides, you smoke too much—you didn't eat a thing!" I sounded just like Aunt Nell, and I knew I was talking into the wind for all the good it would do, but it didn't seem to bother Laney.

"Ah, well," she said, smiling, and took a long, leisurely draw, exhaling slowly before putting the cigarette out. "Amanda wants me to meet her," she said, turning to me.

"Oh, come on, Laney! What's all this about?" I asked as we pulled back into the road.

"You'll see." Laney drove with her right arm across the back of the seat, and a mysterious little smile played on her face. She drove with a kind of cautious flair, her eyes on the rain-slick road ahead. We were in my car because it had been parked behind hers in the driveway, but I was only too eager to let someone else have the wheel.

I began to regret this when she turned into the road that led to Crybaby Bridge. "Why are we going this way?" I asked.

Laney laughed, and I didn't like the way it sounded. "I told you, Amanda wants me to meet her."

"Don't be silly, Laney! You know I don't like this place, especially at night in the rain."

"There's something I have to do," she said. "Please stay with me, Laura."

"Does it have anything to do with Amanda?"

"In a way." Laney's voice was quiet, almost soothing. "You haven't heard the last of Amanda, Laura. Don't forget about her."

"What do you mean?" I knew my response was sharp, but I didn't like being the butt of my cousin's joke, especially on a nasty night anywhere near Crybaby Bridge.

"Don't be so impatient, Laura, it doesn't suit you," my cousin said. "Just promise you won't forget." In the darkness we had come upon the bridge without my knowing it. The ancient timbers rattled beneath the car. I held my breath, waiting impatiently to get to the other side.

Instead the car slowed, stopped. "Why are you stopping? Go on, Laney, please!"

"Wait a minute. Listen!" She rolled the window all the way down. "You can hear the water below and above us. It's singing to us, Laura."

"Please, Laney, let's go!" I wanted to curl up on the floor of the car and hide. I hated being there, hated Laney for doing this to me.

The engine was running, but Laney had taken her foot off the accelerator. I lunged for the wheel and put my foot on the gas. She wasn't expecting it. The car shot forward, scraped against the metal girder, and skidded on the wet bridge when Laney slammed on the brakes.

I slumped on the seat when we stopped. What was going on here? I heard Laney open the car door on the driver's side, heard the scream of the wind. "It's okay, we just bumped the side," she said. "Laura, we have to talk."

I gritted my teeth. "Then get me off this damn bridge! What's wrong with you, Laney? You just about killed us." I clamped my hands together to keep them from shaking.

She laughed as if she hadn't heard me. "Remember that night I broke up with Austin? Remember when I climbed the girders?"

I nodded, afraid to speak, afraid she might do it again.

"There's something I never told you about Austin, Laura." She giggled and whispered in my ear, "Confession time. That year of our junior prom, he was going to ask you."

If I hadn't been so scared, I would have laughed. My cousin had stranded us in this godawful place to tell me about something that happened in high school.

"I told him you were going with somebody else so he would invite me," she said. "I wanted him, Laura, so I took him." Her hand was cold on my arm. "I'm sorry about that, but it's not too late, you know."

"It's okay, I forgive you," I said. I didn't forgive her, though, and I had to clench my teeth to keep from screaming, which was what I thought she wanted me to do. I leaned back against the seat and exhaled slowly, pretending I wasn't afraid. If I could placate Laney, deceive her into letting her guard down, maybe I could get us both off the bridge.

She sat there for a minute staring in my direction, but not seeing me. I had never known my cousin to be like this.

"Come on, let's go home and get something hot to drink," I said softly. When she didn't respond, I made the mistake of grabbing for the car keys.

She was out the door in a second, running down the length of the bridge. I started after her; if it had been daylight, I could have seen the water between the boards, but I knew it was there, foaming, raging, leaping at me.

Something gave inside me, and every wrong, real or imagined, that Laney had ever done me seemed magnified a thousand times. "You're cruel, Laney!" I shouted after her. "Selfish and cruel! You never think of anybody but yourself!" My words seemed to ricochet off the water.

Laney leaned over the side, the keys dangling in her hand. I snatched at them, clawed wildly at my cousin's clothing. "No, Laney no! Please don't—"

My head rang with the scream. Austin, his mother, and his father sat and stared at me as the three bears must have stared at Goldilocks. Austin's mother was crying, silently crying, just as I was. His father was trying not to. "She was gone," I said. "She threw down the keys and just disappeared. I don't know if she jumped or fell, or if I—"

Austin's father stood and paced the length of the room. "But why? For God's sake, why?"

"I don't know." I felt as if I had suffered a long illness. "I hit my head when I fell; I think I must have passed out, and when I woke I was confused. Laney was gone, and the keys were beside me. Her jacket, the purple one she wore so much, was in the car where she'd left it—still dry. She hadn't even worn it.

"All I had was a flashlight, but I tried to search the water. I screamed and called her name—" I broke off. "I thought—I thought maybe I had pushed her. I was so scared I didn't know what I was doing, and I was furious with Laney for stopping on that bridge. I thought I had killed her!" I shivered. "But I couldn't! I didn't!"

Austin smiled for the first time since his mother's accusation. "Laura, you feel guilty if you remove the tag from a sofa pillow. You couldn't hurt anyone, especially Laney."

"Was there really a note?" his father asked.

"I never saw it," I told him, "and I don't think anyone else did, either."

"What happened then? How did you get back to Atlanta?" Daisy had made tea, and she passed a cup to me. It was hot and lemony.

"I remember climbing, sliding down to the bank, pushing through underbrush and briars, but I couldn't see a thing, and there was nothing I could do. I drove back to Laney's and called the police, told them I was driving by and thought I saw someone fall or jump from the bridge; and then I called Aunt Nell and told her Laney didn't answer. She thought I was calling from home. The last thing I remember about being there is hanging Laney's coat in her closet—just like she was going to come back and wear it again...."

The hot tea felt good going down, made me feel stronger. "I don't remember anything about driving back to Atlanta, but my shoes were covered in mud, my arms and legs were scratched all over, and there was a gash in my fender that I couldn't explain. I didn't know what had happened. I thought I was losing my mind."

"I suppose you were in a way," Austin said, "or a part of it."

"When Aunt Nell called early the next morning to tell me they had found Laney's body, it came as a complete shock," I said, "just as if I'd never been there."

"As far as I'm concerned, you never were," Daisy said. "I can't see what possible good it would do, and it would just tear your poor aunt's heart to pieces. She thinks Laney's death was an accident. I'm not going to tell her she took her own life."

Austin and his father agreed, and I was grateful for the grief they spared me. Yet doubts still plucked at me, picked worrisome little holes in the happiness I had found with Austin. There were times when I had been jealous of Laney, had resented the effortless way she danced with life to some special music of her own. Was I bitter enough to push my own cousin from Crybaby Bridge? What awful thing had I done?

TWENTY-SEVEN

"AUNT DELIA'S BACK," Austin said when he called me for the third time the next day. "She's been staying with an old college friend, and Mother knew where she was all along, said she needed to get away."

"Good for her!" I didn't tell Austin, but I had already talked with his Aunt Delia, or at least she had talked with me. It had been a stealthy, hurried, one-sided conversation, and I had the definite idea that she was afraid someone might overhear.

"I wish I could see you tonight," Austin said, "but there's an exam tomorrow in this political science course I'm taking. Guess I'll have to get used to studying all over again."

"Aunt Nell and I will spend the time catching up on things," I said. "We really haven't had a chance to be together lately."

And I really did intend to spend time with my aunt—after I met with Delia Squires, but that was something Austin didn't need to know just yet.

"I'll meet you in the rose garden under the willow," his aunt had said when she called. "There's something I want to show you... I've made up my mind." She spoke so low, I could hardly understand her. "Wait until dusk; if I can't be there, I'll leave a message. And Laura," she added, "try not to let anyone see you."

That was easier said than done, I thought that night as I poked about through waist-high brambles on my clandestine errand. I had parked my car behind Laney's cottage and splashed myself with insect repellent before charging up the hill that separated the two properties. I felt like a cross between Teddy Roosevelt and Nancy Drew, lacking only a pith helmet and a magnifying glass, and I must have looked something like a scarecrow in my long-tailed shirt and faded jeans with a bright bandanna around my head. And this time Vesuvius stayed at home.

Aunt Nell had frowned when I left. "Where on earth are you going like that?"

"Berry picking," I said, rummaging in the cabinet for a bucket. "There are some bushes behind Laney's just loaded with blackberries, and I've been hungry for a cobbler."

"But isn't it kind of late?"

"It's cooler now, and we don't need many." I hurried away. "I won't be long."

I picked as I went along, following the creek through the woods. Berries thudded on the bottom of the pail until it was about half full and my fingers were stained with purple.

Crouching in high grass, I watched the sunset over Willowbend. It would be easy to cut across the pinestudded hill that edged the Squires land. If anyone saw me, I would simply explain that I was picking berries and didn't realize the time. Once inside the rose garden, I would be safe from observation, I thought.

I saw someone moving across the lighted sitting-room window of the Squires home—possibly the judge or Nevin. When the dark hedge blended with the shadows around it, I crept forward, bucket in hand, sounding like a platoon of Weight Watcher dropouts. Every brittle twig in the country broke under my feet; every pebble rolled. Any minute I expected the judge to come running out and pepper me with buckshot, but nothing stirred.

The gate to the garden creaked, of course, and I shut it quickly behind me. There was still enough light to see, so I followed the winding path to the center, almost giddy with the cloying scent of the roses. The bushes were edged with a faint silver sheen that gave me the peculiar illusion that I was walking into a fantasy.

The bench, concealed beneath trailing branches, was empty, but it was still not quite dark; maybe Miss Delia was waiting to be sure she wasn't being followed.

I looked about me and saw no one—not even a leaf stirred in the evening air—but I felt as if I were not alone. Still clutching the pail of berries, I wandered into the protective shadows of the tree and stood with my back against the trunk. If anyone approached, I would be able to see them from there. But no one did, not even Delia Squires.

And then I noticed the book. She had said she would leave a message if she couldn't meet me, and a small book lay on the bench, almost obscured by darkness. On a slip of paper wedged inside she had written one word: *cabin*.

Apparently Delia had felt she was being watched, too. There was no way to get out of the garden without being seen unless I crawled among the roses carrying the bucket in my teeth, which I was definitely not going to do. If someone watched, then let them! I would try to elude them once I got past the hedge.

Leaving the garden behind, I worked my way up the hill the way I had come, sliding on pine needles, darting from bush to bush. A narrow path wound through the dark ravine on the other side, and I had trouble seeing even a few feet in front of me. The remains of the cabin lay just beyond a slight ridge. Was Delia Squires waiting there?

Sweat trickled down my back, and my jeans clung to my legs. In spite of my precautions, mosquitoes buzzed about me: I had hooked a small flashlight to my belt, and it bumped against my hips as I walked, but I was afraid to turn it on. Now and then I thought I heard a slight noise in the darkness behind me, but I wasn't going to stop to find out what it was. I didn't want to know.

The cabin was a black hull leaning into the side of a hill. I could make out the outline of its tilting porch in the gray light. Was I expected to go inside? The porch moaned as I stepped on it, and I whiffed the dry, nose-tickling smell of the fodder stored there. The unmistakable scamper of tiny mouse feet rattled across the floor, and my responding gasp sounded as loud as a scream. Maybe there were rats!

I weighed this possibility against the chance of being followed and switched on the flashlight. It was a good thing I did. Something large and square lay propped against the door frame. If I had not used the light, I might have missed it. I didn't have to guess what it was: Miss Delia's scrapbook.

With coordination I didn't know I had, I snatched up the book and leaped from the porch, running as soon as my feet hit the ground. The bucket went one way, and the berries another. Someone was behind me!

I don't know which raced faster, my heart or my feet, but I was grateful for the times I had jogged around the track back at Benjamin Smithfield Junior High as I scrambled down the furrowed road to my car.

Behind me, someone skidded on slate rock and a limb slapped into place, but I left him (her?) trailing in the rear as I threw myself into my car and groped for the keys. Thank goodness I didn't have to worry about shifting gears. I was almost out to the road before I remembered to turn on the headlights!

Aunt Nell waited on the porch, nervously shifting her bifocals from one hand to the other. I told her I had taken a wrong turn while berry picking and had had trouble finding the way back. "And I'm afraid I spilled the blackberries," I said a little sadly. I really had been looking forward to a cobbler.

My aunt wanted to talk. I thought she was never going to bed. She wanted to talk about Laney, our growing up together. Another time I would have welcomed it, but not tonight. Tonight I wanted to look at the scrapbook. I could hardly wait to get my hands on it!

When everything was quiet at last, I sneaked it out of my car and up to my room. The yellowed pages were brittle and musty. Inside the maroon, cord-bound covers were the bittersweet memories of a woman's life. I began turning the pages, feeling as if I were invading her privacy. The scrapbook was a poignant record of the highlights of a humdrum existence. Delia's baptism was recorded, and her early birthday parties were lavishly described by the society editor of *The Redpath Tribune*. I leafed through sepia school photographs (Delia Squires had been a dainty, round-cheeked child with a wistful smile), age-spotted programs from piano and dance recitals, and family pictures of women in tailored suits and men in uniform. I recognized a snapshot of the judge standing straight and proud: handsome young Captain Decatur Squires, before he left to serve overseas. The word *Papa* was printed carefully in capital letters beneath. Was the picture made before or after Amanda drowned?

And then I came upon the page Delia Squires had meant for me to find: Amanda's page. Two small school pictures of the little girl, probably made in the first and second grades, were pasted in the upper left-hand corner. She had round, pixie eyes, a wide smile, and a narrow ribbon in her straight brown hair. A larger close-up made later showed her sitting on the kitchen steps of Willowbend with a stuffed toy in her arms. My heart sent a message to my eyes and they blurred with tears as I recognized the small musical lamb. Amanda wore a smocked dress with a Peter Pan collar and a stiff-looking bow in her hair. The lamb, which she clutched to her chest, also wore a bow.

Delia Squires had identified the people in the pictures in her neat, childish hand. *Amanda and me* was written below the snapshot of two little girls standing in front of a school. Another showed a pretty young woman with bobbed hair standing beside Amanda with her hands on her shoulders. The woman was identified as Aunt Ada.

The last picture in the group featured two women and Amanda posing beside a car. *Amanda with Aunt Ada and Cousin Lottie on picnic at Kings Mountain* told me what I wanted to know.

I made myself wait until after breakfast to call Austin and was lucky to catch him before he left for work. "Who's Cousin Lottie?" I asked.

"Who?"

I told him about the scrapbook and how I had found it.

"I think this calls for a family conference," he said. "There's something funny going on out there, and it's time we found out what it's all about."

"No, not yet! Please, Austin, she didn't want anyone else to know I had it—not even you. I gave your aunt my word. Besides, we're close to finding out about Amanda; I can feel it. Maybe Cousin Lottie is the clue we've been looking for—whoever she is, or was."

"Mother would know," Austin said, "but it will be hard to find out without making her suspicious." He sighed. "You know how she is."

I certainly did. "Leave it to me," I told him. "How soon can the three of us get together?"

"Well, I guess we could take her to lunch," he said. "She likes that new restaurant at the mall."

"Good, I'll make reservations."

"But, how are you—"

"You just make a date with your mother," I said. "I'll worry about Cousin Lottie."

I wish I felt as confident as I sounded. It was going to be next to impossible to put anything over on Daisy Leatherwood. She gave me a kind of curious look during the drive to the restaurant, and I knew she must be wondering why her son had suddenly decided to treat her to lunch. But from the looks of Daisy, she was never one to turn down a meal.

Austin insisted on ordering a carafe of white wine, and I hoped it would help to put his mother into a receptive mood. I waited until she had sipped about half a large glass before I asked, "Mrs. Leatherwood, didn't your father have a sister named Lottie?"

I thought Austin was going to ram an entire breadstick down his throat.

"Lottie?" Raised eyebrows, but no obvious suspicion—so far. "Why no, there was just Papa and Aunt Ada, but she died when she was young."

"Aunt Nell and I were talking about names at supper last night—old-fashioned names you never hear anymore, like Lottie—and she said she thought you had an aunt by that name."

"Oh, well of course! She must have meant Cousin Lottie." She dumped Thousand Island dressing onto her salad, eyeing it eagerly. "She wasn't really our cousin, just a family friend. She and my grandmother grew up together."

"Hm, never heard of her. What happened to her?" Austin salted his salad twice.

"Well, my goodness, Austin, I suppose the woman's long dead. She was the same age as my grandmother, which would make her over a hundred now!'' Daisy crammed lettuce into her mouth and chewed it thoroughly.

"You're not talking about Lottie Hucks, are you?'' I asked. (I *had* heard my aunt speak of a Lottie Hucks.)

Daisy swallowed. "No, no, Lottie Maxwell. Lived over in Bishopville, had a daughter named Betty Jane—no, Betty Ann.'' She frowned. "They used to come to see us some when I was little.... Wonder what happened to Betty Ann.''

Bishopville. Austin kicked me under the table. I rubbed my shin. "Maybe she still lives there,'' I said. "She's probably a grandmother by now.''

"My goodness, I hadn't thought of that girl in ages,'' Austin's mother said. "She was a right pretty girl, about five or six years older than I was. Last time I saw her she must've been eighteen or twenty.''

"Where did you say Cousin Lottie lived?'' Austin asked as we drove home.

His mother gave him a funny look. "In Bishopville, over in Lee County. Why all the sudden interest in somebody you never heard of before today?''

He shrugged. "Just curious.''

"I went to school with a girl from Bishopville,'' I said quickly. "Pretty little town.''

Daisy dug into her pocketbook for a compact and powdered her nose. "Hm, how about that?'' she said. Austin held the door for her as she stepped from the car. She turned at her front door and smiled at us. "You two be sure and let me know if you find out anything!'' And she wiggled her fingers at us before going inside.

"She knows,'' I said.

"She suspects,'' Austin corrected me, smiling. "Don't let her fool you.''

I was quiet for the short drive back to Aunt Nell's.
Something badgered me, something Austin's mother had
said. Suddenly I leaned forward, straining at my seat belt.
"I've got it!" I yelled. "It's Lee *County*! Remember, your
mother said Bishopville was in Lee County? Well, that
must be what's on the locket; it was engraved with the
name Lee and then a letter C, but there was a dent right
beside it which obliterated the small *o*." I smiled. "Don't
you see? Amanda was actually born in Lee County!"

Austin grinned. "No, I don't see, but I'm willing to listen." He followed me up the steps to the porch. "Only this
time take it a little slower, okay?" Austin glanced at the
box by the door. "Mail's come."

We reached for it at the same time. The letter was on
top, again addressed to me. This time Laney had written
her message on an index card:

> "DYING IS AN ART, LIKE EVERYTHING ELSE."
> "I DO IT EXCEPTIONALLY WELL."

Austin snatched up the envelope. "It's her handwriting, all right; I'm sure of it. And it's postmarked Bishopville."

"This sounds familiar," I said. "I've heard it somewhere before."

"It has quotation marks around it...." Austin shrugged.
"Don't ask me!"

"Of course! Sylvia Plath!"

"Sylvia who?" Austin looked blank.

"The poet Sylvia Plath," I explained. "Laney wrote her
term paper on her, remember? And just before she died,
she checked out one of her books from the library."

Austin examined the card again and stuffed it back into
the envelope. "I hope you don't have any big plans for to-

morrow," he told me, "because we're going on a little trip."

"To Bishopville," I said.

He slapped the envelope against his hand. "To Bishopville."

TWENTY-EIGHT

"ARE YOU SURE your mother won't mind keeping Will?"
I asked as we left Redpath the next morning. Somehow I
couldn't imagine Daisy Leatherwood entertaining a two-
year-old all day.

Austin stroked the back of my neck with his fingers. A
sensitive place, the back of the neck; I moved a little closer.
"She raised me, didn't she?" he asked. "Don't worry, he'll
be fine."

My aunt had a dental appointment in Columbia and
would be gone most of the day, and I had agreed earlier to
stay with Will. Austin's mother offered to pinch hit for me
when he convinced her we needed to go out of town.

"Do you think she knows where we're going?" I asked,
wondering if I had left Will enough extra clothes. So far,
he had been resistant to toilet training.

"I'm sure she knows where," he said, "and knowing my
mother, it's only a matter of time before she finds out
why."

Austin had insisted on driving his truck, and I rolled
down the window and let the cool morning air rush past as
the road unwound beneath us. I closed my eyes and smiled,
knowing he was there beside me. I could ride on like this
forever, I thought, if our lives were not so full of ghosts:
ghosts of my dead cousin and of a child we had never seen.

"I'm not sure Laney's dead, Laura," Austin said, as if
he could read my thoughts. He spoke slowly, softly, yet it
jarred me from my musings. "This is just like something

she would do: send us off on a wild-goose chase, a bizarre treasure hunt!"

"Laney would never leave Will if she were alive," I argued. "Besides, the message was plain. Laney's dead, Austin. I think she killed herself."

"What message? Oh, you mean the last one about dying being an art?" He didn't sound convinced.

"Sylvia Plath's message, and Laney's," I said. "Sylvia Plath killed herself, too. Stuck her head in a gas oven."

He shuddered. "But why Laney? No one loved living more than she did, Laura. What would make her do a thing like that?"

"I don't know," I said. "Maybe we'll find out in Bishopville; maybe Betty Ann will tell us, if there is a Betty Ann."

For an answer he took my hand and kissed it, then held it in his lap. He doesn't believe in Betty Ann, either, I thought.

We drove through flat pine land and cottonfields, where long rows of the tender green plants stretched out of sight. The two-lane road dipped through a cool tunnel of trees as we crossed the Little Lynches River, then rose slightly until we turned into the main street of Bishopville.

Past the red-brick middle school, neat, freshly painted cottages lined both sides of the street, and closer to town we saw older, statelier homes, graceful tokens of another time, that sat back from the road.

"Where do we go first?" I asked as we passed through the clean, uncluttered business district of the little town. "There's the courthouse over there!" I pointed out a large cream-colored brick building with granite pillars.

"I think the post office is our best bet," Austin said, asking directions from a lady in the parking lot of the grocery store across the street.

I prayed to myself as we walked into the building. I was ready for this nightmare to be over, and I needed all the help I could get. But the young clerk had never heard of Lottie Maxwell or her daughter Betty Ann. "I've only been working here a few months," she explained. "Let me ask Mr. Sutherland in the back; he might know."

Mr. Sutherland was a wiry little man with a bristling moustache who looked to be in his early sixties. "Well, of course I remember Miss Lottie," he said. "She taught me in Sunday school for years." He polished his glasses and held them to the light. "My goodness, I guess she's been dead fifteen or twenty years now."

"She had a daughter, Betty Ann," Austin said. "Does she still live around here?"

"Well, I reckon she does!" Satisfied with his glasses, Mr. Sutherland put them back on and winked at me. "We went to school together, but she'll try to tell you she's younger than I am. She still lives in the old home place. It's only a few blocks from here.... Name's Darnell now, Betty Ann Darnell...married Howard Darnell. Runs that feed store down past the silos."

We thanked him after getting directions and hurried to the car. "If Betty Ann talks as much as her friend at the post office, it ought to solve all our problems," I said. I tried to make lighthearted conversation, but I felt far from frivolous. If our hunch about Betty Ann didn't work out, we would face a dead end.

We turned off Church Street and drove past the big yellow cotton gin through quiet streets shaded by large oaks. The old Maxwell home was of a type Aunt Nell would call a Sand Hills cottage, a simple story and a half with three dormer windows above a long front porch. A narrow brick walk curved through a lawn bordered with holly and azaleas, and a large redbud tree shaded the front steps. I didn't blame Betty Ann for remaining in this place.

A slender, sweet-faced woman in a white tennis dress answered the door. Her light hair blended with gray, and her face was flushed, as if she had just come from the courts.

Austin took the initiative. "Mrs. Darnell? Betty Ann Darnell?"

"Yes?" She ran a hand loosely through her short hair.

"I don't know how to say this...." He looked helplessly from the woman at the door to me, then back again. "I'm—uh, Austin Leatherwood, and this is—"

"Laura Graham," I said. "We just drove over from Redpath, and—"

The woman smiled and pushed open the door, inviting us inside. "Well, it's about time," she said. "I wondered when you were coming."

We followed her into a dim hallway, where a large bowl of magnolia leaves stood on a walnut console table.

"I have a letter for you," she told me. "I was to mail it in a week if you didn't show up by then." She led us to a small sitting room just off the kitchen and stood on tiptoe to remove a book from the shelf. "I kept them in this old book. It was a present to my mother from Ada Squires." She smiled at Austin, gesturing for us to be seated. "She was your great-aunt, I believe? I knew your mother, but I haven't seen her in years. You look very much like your grandfather."

The book was a leatherbound volume of poetry with gold embossed lettering. From it Betty Ann Darnell took a fat business-size envelope, already stamped and addressed to me in Laney's hand.

I frowned. I was tired of playing games. "Where did you get this?" I demanded. "Who asked you to do this, and why?"

She sat across from us, her tanned arms resting on the stark white skirt. "She came to see me in early March, and she said her name was Laney McCall; I had no reason to doubt her. She was tall and blond and very beautiful, but there was a sadness about her, a kind of an ache in her eyes."

"She came here about Amanda," she said, "traced me through a scrapbook—Cousin Delia Squires's, I think." Betty Ann clasped her hands together and looked from Austin to me. "Something seemed to bother her about the way Amanda died. She said she wanted to learn the truth."

I held the thick envelope, unopened, on my lap. "And did she?"

She shook her head. "I don't know. I think she meant for you to do that for her."

Our hostess moved lightly into the kitchen; I heard her tossing ice into glasses. "She said it was a game," she told us, serving mint-sprigged glasses of tea. "A kind of treasure hunt, and I've always liked adventure, so I agreed to help her out."

The small woman sat on the arm of a chair, the empty tray across her lap. "She told me she had to go away for a while and was afraid she wouldn't have time to find out before she . . . left."

She smiled at me, but her eyes were sad. "You were to take up where she left off, and I was to send you the reminders, one at a time, beginning in mid-June and mailing them a week apart.

"She was lying about leaving, of course." Her long fingers tapped the tray. "She's dead, isn't she?"

I nodded. "Yes, Laney's dead. Now, can you tell us about Amanda?"

"She was born here in Bishopville, in this house." Betty Ann opened a drawer to a desk in the corner. "This is her birth certificate," she said, giving it to me. "Her mother left it here for safe-keeping. I was only twelve at the time, but I remember the night she was born."

I studied the paper in my hand. "Ada Squires *was* Amanda's mother!" I told Austin. "But why are there two birth certificates?"

Our hostess pointed to a signature at the bottom of the page. "This was signed by old Dr. Renfroe, who delivered her. He used to live next door; and there's a copy on file at the courthouse downtown."

Austin frowned. "And I guess my honorable great-grandfather, Colonel Porter Squires, lied to the doctor in Redpath, told him the baby was born to that awful Scoggins woman. One baby, two birth certificates. No one checked, or even cared."

"Until now," I said, "and only because of the locket. Ada Squires wanted Amanda to know her real birth certificate was on file here in Lee County, so she had it engraved on the locket."

"I think she meant for Amanda to inherit her share of her father's estate," Betty Ann said. "She couldn't know the child would die soon after she did."

Ada Squires had come there, she told us, as soon as her father had learned she was pregnant. The baby's father had since left town, and Lottie Maxwell, a close family friend, lived far enough away that no one would ever know. When Amanda was born, she was given to the Scogginses to raise so Ada would always be close enough to keep an eye on her.

"Of course I was told this much later," Betty Ann confessed. "Back then, we didn't discuss such things as having babies out of wedlock. I was told Cousin Ada 'wasn't feeling well,' and I wasn't even supposed to know when Amanda was born." She laughed. "I did, of course. We had more sense back then than they gave us credit for."

"I want you to keep the birth certificate," she said as we got ready to leave. "And whatever you learn about Amanda, I'd be glad if you'd let me know. We used to visit there when I was young, and she was a delightful little girl."

"Do you think there was anything peculiar about the way she died?" I asked.

"I didn't know about it until later," she admitted. "Mother told me it was an accident, and she had no reason to think otherwise." Betty Ann Darnell followed us to the door. "I'm sorry to hear about Laney, although I'm not surprised," she said. "She must have been very special."

I looked at Austin and smiled. "She was," I admitted.

TWENTY-NINE

"I'M HUNGRY," Austin announced as we drove slowly through the center of town. "See if you can find a place to eat."

I didn't answer. How could he possibly think of food? At that moment I had no room in my thoughts for anything but the envelope in my lap. My happiness depended on it, mine and Austin's.

He stopped at a roadside ice cream stand, where a hand-lettered sign also advertised sandwiches and home-fried okra, and insisted on having lunch. Since it would have been useless to argue, I ordered a milk shake.

Austin considered his hot dog from both ends. "Well," he said, "aren't you going to read Laney's letter?"

"Not here. Not now." I turned to him and was surprised at the tremor in my voice. "Austin, do you mind very much if I read it alone?" I knew this would be my last time to be with Laney. It was addressed to me, and I didn't want to share it, not yet.

"No, of course not. But surely you aren't planning to wait until we get back to Redpath? Laura, aren't you even curious?"

I smiled. "More than curious. There's a bench under a shade tree back there in front of that church we passed. If I could just sit there by myself for a few minutes, I'd be ready to start back home."

"You've got it." Austin turned the car around. "I need to fill up the gas tank anyway. I'll come back for you in a little while."

I sat on the cool stone bench and watched him drive away, the envelope heavy in my hand. Across the street two little girls laughed as they raced their bikes; one was dark, the other fair. . . .

I slit open the envelope and began to read.

Dear Laura,

I can just see you now. You're furious with me, aren't you, for shoving you "head-first and blind-folded" into a real-life game of *Clue*, for making a game of death? Well, I'd much rather live, but if I can't be the life of the party, I'd just as soon go home. I found out a few weeks ago I have lung cancer, Laura, and if everything goes as I've planned, you'll be with me at the end. I need the comfort of your love to do what I have to do, and I hope you'll forgive me. I hope you'll understand.

Amanda was real, as you probably know by now if you've followed all my leads. Find out for me, if you can, exactly how she died. I'm not satisfied with what I've learned, and I'm running out of time. Someone at Willowbend knows more than they're willing to tell, and I think there's danger there, so be careful!

I hope that by now you and Austin have found each other again. Aside from that crazy last year in high school, I don't think he's ever really cared for any-one else. (And admit it, Laura, if you were in love with that counselor guy, you'd have married him by now!)

I'm gambling that your concern, (and, yes, guilt—I know you) over my death will bring you back home and keep you there long enough to follow through. I've been blamed for overshadowing you, and maybe it's true; I didn't mean to. Now it's your time to shine.

Can you feel me there shaking you, prodding you from behind? Wake up, Laura! Don't wait too long at the fair. And remember not to swat any butterflies!

I really do love you,

Laney

I sat there like an idiot, laughing through my tears. Laney had always said that if there was such a thing as reincarnation, she wanted to come back as a butterfly.

I was still smiling when Austin drew up in front of me, and I hurried to get in beside him.

"Are you all right?" He looked me over carefully before pulling away from the curb.

"I think I'm going to be fine," I said. "Would you like for me to read you Laney's letter?"

"It will be a long walk back if you don't," he said.

Laney had enclosed two letters in the envelope; the other, still sealed, I was to keep for Will until he was old enough to understand. My letter was dated only a few days before Laney died.

Austin's face was thoughtful as I read. "What do you think she meant, 'There's danger at Willowbend'? Sounds melodramatic to me."

"Laney *was* melodramatic," I said. "You're talking about a person who's manipulated this whole performance from beyond the grave. Remember when you said those messages sounded just like something Laney would do?"

He nodded. "And we were a part of that plan, Laura, you and me. Do you mind?"

I kissed his cheek. "What do you think?" Still, I had to admit, what my cousin had said about danger bothered me, bothered me a lot.

"There's something I haven't told you," I confessed, "something about your Aunt Delia." Austin groaned when I told him how his aunt had taken the things from my room the night she disappeared.

"But she stayed with my parents that night!" he said. "Mother took her to the airport the next morning."

"I'm not saying she didn't spend the night there," I said, "but I'll be willing to bet she didn't get there until after dark."

"But why would she drop that flower to make you think it was Uncle Nevin?"

"I don't know, but if I can ever get your aunt to come out of hiding, I intend to find out."

I leaned back against the seat, and it descended on me like a hundred little spider legs crawling along my spine—the same irrational terror I had experienced when I turned on my answering machine back in March and heard Laney's chilling words, "I'm meeting Amanda tomorrow night at Crybaby Bridge." She'd had a note from her, she said when I returned her call, and I agreed to come on my way home from the teachers' workshop.

"Not a word to anybody," she said. "Promise you won't tell!"

And I agreed. I would agree to anything to keep her off that bridge.

But it didn't help. My stomach plunged. Something awful was going to happen!

"Isn't there a filling station a few miles down the road?" I asked after we had been driving almost an hour.

"Um-hum, little country crossroads. Why?"

"I want to call your mother, see if Will's okay. Please, Austin I'm afraid something's terribly wrong!" I was getting sick, physically sick. Will was in danger, I knew it, and I was still over an hour away.

"Sure, no problem. I could use a soft drink, anyway."
Austin must have sensed the depth of my fear. "But
Mother isn't going to like it when I wake Will from his afternoon nap just to tell her we're on our way." His smile
was reassuring.

"You can blame it on me," I said as we pulled into the
station.

He went inside and came out with two Cokes, passing
one through the window to me. I stepped down from the
truck and followed him to the phone booth next to the
road, holding the cold can with both hands. A moist gust
of wind rattled a discarded paper cup across the pave-
ment, and I noticed the sun had disappeared behind a
smear of clouds.

I knew from his face that something was wrong when
Austin stepped from the phone booth.

"That was Dad," he explained, hurrying me back to the
truck. "He just dropped by the house for a sandwich.
Mother's not there, but she left a note: she's taken Will to
Willowbend."

THIRTY

I BRACED MYSELF against the dashboard as we careened into the highway. "Hey, watch it, or we won't get back at all!" I said in what I hoped was a reasonable voice. "I'm sure Will's okay, or your mother wouldn't have left him there."

Nevin Squires had had car trouble on his way to Greenville for a meeting, the note said, and he had called asking Daisy to come and get him. Since she didn't want to drag Will along, she had turned to her sister for help.

"Why didn't Nevin ask Delia or the judge to come for him?" I asked.

"Aunt Delia hasn't driven outside of Redpath in years," Austin explained. "She's terrified of strange places, and it's Grandfather's day at the golf course; nothing interferes with that. Besides," he added, "I doubt if Uncle Nevin would want his father to know he needed help of any kind. It would be a sign of weakness."

Although I clung to my seat belt and pressed my foot against the floorboard, I was just as eager to get back as Austin. What kind of people were his relatives? And little Will was at Willowbend completely at their mercy.

Delia Squires seemed perfectly harmless, but she had knocked me down on the dark stairs after burglarizing my room and had led me on a frightening chase to find her scrapbook in the old cabin. I wondered if it had been Delia who had searched Laney's cottage before I found the locket. Except for small details, the house had been tidy, as someone like Miss Delia might have left it.

Again, I found myself becoming angry with my cousin for dumping all this in my lap and taking the short way out. If she hadn't taken her own life, she would probably still be alive. Why, people lived for months with lung cancer, maybe even years.

"I wonder why the local doctor didn't say anything about Laney having cancer when all this happened," I said.

"Laney didn't go to the local doctor. She went to somebody in Columbia. I remember her telling me she had an appointment for a physical back in February." Austin frowned. "I never asked her the outcome; I just assumed she was okay."

"But I know there was an autopsy. They told Aunt Nell she drowned. Wouldn't the pathologist have discovered the cancer as well?"

"I'm sure he did, and it's probably in the coroner's report, but remember who the coroner is, Laura: Raymond Peeler. Isn't he kinda sweet on your Aunt Nell?"

"Just friends really, but they go out now and then to Rotary dances and such. He and Aunt Nell were classmates, and I know he's fond of her."

"He wouldn't want her to know Laney committed suicide; I think he'd try to spare her that," Austin said, "and if he told her about the cancer, she would have known without a doubt. Besides, as far as we know, no one actually saw Laney jump—not even you."

Austin slowed as we passed through another small village, then picked up speed on the other side. Scenery whizzed past; trees, fields, and sky became a greenish-gray blur. Then finally I recognized the familiar water tower on the outskirts of Redpath. We were almost home.

Skies were darkening as we turned into the long, grim drive at Willowbend, and wind rustled the thick hedge as we got out of the truck and ran to the house. The place looked more forbidding than ever and seemed to be deserted.

We didn't bother to knock but went right inside. The door was unlocked, but no lights burned in the cavernous downstairs hall.

"Aunt Delia? Will?" Austin turned on lights as we circled the first floor, calling out all the while. It was after four o'clock, and Will should be awake from his nap.

"Shouldn't your grandfather be home from the golf course?" I asked. "It looks like we're in for a storm."

"Not if he decides to stay for dinner," Austin said. "And if there's a bridge game going on, he probably won't be home before dark."

"Are you sure your dad said Will was here? Where could they have gone?" We stood in the dimly lit hall, while outside tall pines dipped in the wind.

"Wait, be quiet!" Austin gripped my arm. "I hear something upstairs, a knocking sound."

We raced up the steps following the noise, which sounded like a shutter rapping in the wind. It seemed to be coming from the third floor.

Breathing heavily, I clung to the newel post as Austin swung past me into the dingy hallway. "It's the wardrobe!" I shouted. "Someone's in the wardrobe!"

"Please help me! Let me out!" Delia's voice was weak and frightened. How long had she been inside? And where was Will?

My foot hit something metallic as I ran toward the wardrobe, and a small object skidded across the floor.

"It's the key!" Austin scooped it up, fumbling to unlock the heavy oak door. He caught his tiny aunt as she tumbled out, and we carried her gently downstairs.

"Thank goodness you've come," she sighed as her nephew made her comfortable on the sofa and placed a damp towel on her head. Her small face was pink and wet with perspiration, and her hair clung to her forehead in sticky strands.

"Where is Will?" I asked as Austin hurried in with a glass of water for his aunt. "I thought he was here with you."

She drank the water thirstily, and her body shook with coughing. "He took him!" she cried, leaning back against the cushions. "I couldn't stop him. He's gone completely crazy—locked me in the wardrobe and went off with that little boy!"

"Who? Who did this to you?" Austin demanded, but I think he already knew the answer.

"Why, Nevin," she answered, "your Uncle Nevin!" She grasped my hand in both of hers. "He wants you to wait here until he calls.... Oh, what are we going to do?"

Austin waited as she took another sip, while I fanned her with the morning paper. "Where's Mother, Aunt Delia?" he asked. "Take your time and start at the beginning. We need to know everything."

Miss Delia sat up straighter and dropped the towel to the floor. "Your mother's out looking for Nevin. She thinks he had car trouble this side of Greenville. He didn't, of course; he only wanted her out of the way. It was a trick to get her to bring the boy here."

"But why?" I asked.

"He wants you, Laura. He's using the child as bait," she explained.

"I don't understand!" In an instant I was across the room, one hand on the telephone. "Will he hurt him? Should we call the police?" It was hard for me to believe that the gentle librarian I had always known had turned my whole world upside down.

"I don't think he'll hurt the child," she said. "He has no reason to, and I don't want to risk upsetting him more. At least wait until he calls."

Wait? How could I wait while a madman had our Will? This woman was trying to pacify someone with an unbalanced mind; yet I had no idea where Nevin Squires could be. I had no choice but to wait: to sit in this ugly, dismal old house and wait for his call.

Austin drew me to him and stood with an arm about my shoulders as his aunt told her story, beginning with the day I found the scrapbook.

Nevin had been upset with her since she had led me to the scrapbook, she told us. He had followed her to the rose garden that night, but she evaded him, leaving a note in the book to tell me to come to the cabin. Rather than pursue his sister, Nevin Squires waited for me and followed me through the woods, hoping I would lead him to his sister's scrapbook, but I was more agile than he gave me credit for, and he couldn't come out of hiding without giving himself away.

"He came home at noon today, furious with me because Daisy had told him you two were on your way to Bishopville to see Lottie Maxwell's daughter," Delia said. "Of course Daisy didn't know why, but Nevin did, and so did I. 'It's all your fault,' he said. 'They wouldn't have known about Lottie if it hadn't been for that scrapbook of yours!'"

"I found out later he'd gone back to the library and called Daisy, pretending to need a ride home from somewhere near Greenville. When she came by here later with Will, she just said Nevin was having car trouble, but she didn't say where, so I didn't think much about it."

Delia's eyes filled with tears. "I'd just gotten him down for his nap when Nevin came back—locked me in the wardrobe and left with the child." She touched my arm lightly. "I don't think he woke. I didn't hear him crying."

"What's so important about our going to Bishopville?" Austin asked. "And why should Uncle Nevin care?"

His aunt threw her head back and breathed deeply. "Because he doesn't want anyone to know about Amanda—who she was—or what he did."

"But what—" I began, but Delia didn't hear me, or if she did she decided to answer in her own good time.

"I'm sorry about taking those things from your aunt's house that night," she said. "I hope I didn't hurt you on the stairs.... I was so frightened.... All I wanted was to get out without being seen. Nevin bullied me into doing it, threatened to tell Papa about some things I did when I was younger. I got away after that night, someplace where I could think clearly. I had to make up my mind. I don't care what Nevin says or what Papa thinks. I can't hold this back any longer."

"You left the rosebud," I reminded her.

She nodded. "I wanted you to think it was Nevin; after all, he was behind it. He had to have Amanda's locket, he said, and her poor little lamb; and of course you had asked about that library reminder, and he wanted that as well." She stood slowly and went to the window, where a pyracantha scraped against the glass. "I know he searched Laney's house trying to find it after she died."

"But how did he know I had the lamb?" I asked.

"I guess that's my fault," Austin admitted. "I mentioned it to him, thinking he might know where it came from."

"He has Amanda's things in his room," Delia told me. "I'll see that you get them back."

I thanked her, remembering Goldie Lee. "I know someone who would love to have them," I said. "And speaking of the music box, do you know anything about my being locked out on the cupola the day of the class picnic?"

"Nevin," she said quietly. "He was trying to scare you away. He denied it, of course, but I saw him coming from the attic with that lamb—Amanda's lamb! He had found it earlier in some of her things, and I'm afraid he might've used it to mislead Laney. I saw him coming from the cabin with it one evening back in the winter; of course I had no idea what he was doing until later!"

Her fingers plucked at the curtains. "I knew Nevin was up to something poking about in that sweltering attic the day of the picnic," she added. "I was on my way to see what was going on when Austin heard you calling for help." Miss Delia pressed her forehead against the window. "I should've done something then, should have made a stand long ago, but—"

The screeching of tires outside brought me to my feet, and I jumped as the front door slammed. "I've been all the way around Robin Hood's barn," Daisy Leatherwood bellowed, "and there's no sign of that fool Nevin or his car! What's going on here?"

Austin went quickly to meet his mother in the hall, and I heard her rumbling voice rise in shock, then Austin's soothing replies.

I took advantage of his absence to ask another question. "Miss Delia," I began "that night in the cemetery, the night Amanda came . . . was that you?"

She smiled as her eyes met mine. "Amanda? What night was this?"

"It was the Sunday I was here with Austin. You gave me the roses, remember?· Later that night I was at Laney's packing some of her things when I heard the music box again."

She seemed genuinely shocked. "And you think that I would do a cruel thing like that?"

"Then who? Surely not Nevin! I saw—"

But she was shaking her head. "No. It couldn't have been Nevin that night. The quartet he sings with rehearsed here for an anthem they're singing the Fourth of July. It was a special treat for me because we seldom have company, and Papa and I sat and listened the whole time." Delia smiled remembering. "It was 'America the Beautiful.' That's Papa's favorite, you know, and I served refreshments afterward, of course."

Then who had I followed to the cemetery?

"But you wanted me to learn about Amanda," I said. "Isn't that why you led me to the scrapbook?"

She nodded silently and looked away.

"And Laney? You showed it to her, too?"

"Yes. She became curious when she found the locket, and I left my scrapbook where she could find it when she was here one day. She cared, you see, just as I hoped you would."

"But why didn't you say something? Why didn't you tell us?"

She stiffened. "I gave my word. I promised. But that was long ago, and I was wrong. Very wrong. I just couldn't live with it anymore."

"Couldn't live with what anymore?" Daisy's voice boomed as she marched into the room with Austin behind her.

Delia Squires looked calmly up at her sister. "What Nevin did on Crybaby Bridge."

"And what was that?" Daisy demanded. "I think it's time you got away from this gloomy old house, Delia! And where is Nevin, anyway? Austin says he's off with that child somewhere, and it's getting close to suppertime. His aunt will wonder where we are."

Austin shook his head at me over his mother's shoulder. Clearly she didn't understand the seriousness of the situation. And I had almost forgotten about Aunt Nell. What was I going to tell her?

With one small hand, Delia Squires pushed her older sister into a chair. "After all these years, you still don't understand, do you, Daisy? Nevin is sneaky; he's rotten, always has been! And now he's taken Laney's little boy to keep Laura from telling his secret."

Daisy Leatherwood's face turned from a furious red to a sort of bluish white. "What secret? I'll swear, Delia, you've finally popped your cork! What are you babbling about?"

"I'm talking about Amanda," Delia said quietly.

"Amanda? You mean Amanda Scoggins, the little girl who used to live in the cabin?"

Delia nodded. "Amanda was our cousin, Daisy. She was Aunt Ada's child. Nevin and I overheard Grandpa talking about it with cousin Lottie after Aunt Ada died. Remember when Amanda came to live with us? Remember how she died?"

"No, I don't remember how she died," Daisy said. "I was away at camp that summer. And what does it have to do with Nevin?" She looked from Austin to me and finally to Delia. "Papa told me she fell from the bridge and drowned. Isn't that what happened?"

Delia folded her arms and stood with her back against the gray window light. "Not exactly," she said.

When the phone rang, I was the first to reach it. "Meet me at the bridge in fifteen minutes," Nevin Squires said. "Bring Amanda's birth certificate, and come alone!"

I stood with the receiver in my hand as if it were a lifeline to Will. Outside, the first raindrops began to fall. "Will's okay," I told the others. "He spoke to me, but Nevin won't let me have him unless I come alone."

"Then you're a fool," Delia said. "He wants you in the river, too, Laura, and he doesn't want any witnesses!"

THIRTY-ONE

"YOU'RE NOT GOING alone!" Austin shouted as I raced for the door. "Wait, Laura! Use your head!"

His mother slumped in the chair, her eyes staring in disbelief. "Doesn't Nevin know there would be another copy of Amanda's birth certificate on file?" she asked when I repeated what her brother had said. She shook her head slowly. "What good will it do to destroy this one?"

"He's not thinking clearly, Mother," Austin said, touching her shoulder as he passed. "He's left reality behind."

"Nevin doesn't care about the birth certificate," Delia reminded us. "It's Laura he wants!"

I hurried out to the truck and snatched the brittle document from the seat where I had left it. "I'll cut through the cemetery on foot," I told them as they clustered about me in the rain. "If I drive over there, he might think I'm not alone."

"You won't be!" Austin stepped in front of me. "I'm taking the back road to the bridge. I'll park out of sight so he won't know I'm there." He pulled me to him and kissed me briefly. "Nothing's going to happen to you, I won't let it. Don't let him get close to you, Laura. No matter what he does, don't get near him! And remember, I'll be there."

"So will I," his mother said, climbing into the passenger side of the truck.

"Wait, you'll get soaking wet!" Delia threw a yellow rain slicker around me and scrambled up beside her sister. "Move over. I'm coming, too."

I slipped into the raincoat as I ran through a gap in the hedge and across a rough field on the other side. The slicker smelled musty, as if it had been hanging in the back hall closet for years, but it was warm and dry. I pulled the hood over my head as I ran, grateful for its protection.

The pale gravestones huddled in the slanting rain beyond the rusting fence. I skirted the desolate place with a brief glance at the sad little grave in the rear, almost expecting to see an elusive figure in white. Poor Amanda! What had happened to her that day on Crybaby Bridge? And who had led me to her lonely grave?

Stepping carefully through the boggy pine ground, I made my way to the road with Amanda's birth certificate tucked in the pocket of my skirt. The black mud sucked at my feet as I ran, and water streamed down my face. I was glad to reach the solidity of the narrow asphalt road, splashing through puddles as I ran, soaking my bare legs and the hem of my skirt. Will had sounded all right on the phone; soon I would see him, hold him! I ran faster. Had it been more than fifteen minutes? Would they be there when I came?

I saw the framework looming over the trees as I rounded the bend in the road, and suddenly I came upon the bridge itself. And there they were, a splotch of color in the dreary gray center of the bridge. Nevin Squires waited in the rain, his blue-striped tie neatly tucked inside a navy windbreaker, his graying hair slick with rainwater. He had one arm casually around Will who sat on the low girder behind him calmly licking a red lollypop and swinging his short legs. He looked up happily and waved a hand. "Dauwa!" he shouted, swaying.

I stood still in my tracks as Nevin caught him, steadying him on his perch. "Get him down," I said softly. "He doesn't realize the danger."

He smiled a prissy, pompous little smile. "Well now, he's fine as long as you don't frighten him, Laura. I'm not going to let him fall." He held out a hand. "You brought the birth certificate, I hope?"

I nodded mutely, remembering Austin's warning. I hadn't heard the truck approaching, nor did I see a sign of it. Nevin Squires's blue sedan was parked at the far end of the bridge well to the side of the road. I wondered how long he had been there. Above the pounding of the rain and the roar of the river below, I thought I heard a different sound, like the faraway cry of a child in distress. I had heard it once before. I hoped I would never hear it again.

"Your family knows you're here," I said, inching closer one step at a time. "They know what you've done. You can destroy Amanda's birth certificate, but you can't deny her existence."

His smug expression didn't change. "Do you really think my family would abandon me to back your silly claims? Delia will protect me—she gave her word—and so will the rest of them. Amanda's birth was a disgrace, a stain on the family name! No one will listen to you."

Will shivered and made a small whimpering sound. The baggy wool sweater Nevin had thrown around his small shoulders was soggy with rain.

"He's cold," I said, "and wet. Please let him go. You can have the birth certificate." I held it out to him, afraid to move.

But he didn't seem to hear me. "No one listened to your cousin, either, I made sure of that. High-strung girl like that—always was a little different." He laughed. "Nobody would believe a woman who said she heard ghostly music and got notes from a dead person!"

"You left those notes for Laney, the notes she found in the cabin?" I hadn't believed her, either. I thought she had made them up. "Why?"

"To discredit her story, for one thing. I couldn't have her running around reviving old ghosts. If she hadn't found that locket and poked her nose where it didn't belong, none of this would have happened." He leaned against the railing and pulled Will a little closer.

"I only wanted to frighten her that night, give her a little scare," he said. "It was dark when she came to the bridge. . . . I didn't plan on her bringing you."

My breath came like a sharp stab in the chest. "You killed Laney! You pushed her off the bridge!"

"No! No, you're wrong." He held up a hand as if it mattered now what he said. "She never even saw me. I was in the woods back there with a flashlight and a sheet. All I wanted to do was frighten the silly girl, make her wish she'd never heard of Amanda."

He took a folded handkerchief from his pocket and blotted the water from his face. "She never knew I was there. After that scuffle with you, she stood for a second on the side of the bridge and stepped out into nothing: 'a pardlike spirit, beautiful and swift'; then darkness claimed her."

A steely calmness came over me, and I knew he was telling the truth. "Why didn't you help me? We might have saved her."

He gave a slight shake of his head. "It was no use; besides, I don't think your cousin wanted saving."

While we were talking, I had watched Austin and the two women approaching on foot. Now they stood quietly several feet behind Nevin at the far end of the bridge. I kept my eyes on the child in front of me as I spoke. "All that's over, Mr. Nevin. It wasn't your fault. Just let me have Will, and we won't talk about it anymore." I tried to keep my voice expressionless, my face guarded.

He reached abruptly for the paper in my hand. As he did, Will dropped his candy with a cry into the river below and reeled suddenly forward. I covered the distance between us in one step, grabbing him as he fell, sobbing as I felt his cool, wet cheek next to mine.

"Run, Will! Run to Austin!" I shouted, setting him on his feet as Nevin Squires gripped my arm, swinging me about.

"I told you to come alone!" he screamed, backing me against the hard metal scaffolding. I watched almost as a distant observer as Austin swung Will into his arms and passed him along to Daisy while the eerie wailing of the river rose to a startling crescendo.

Nevin's face went white. His hands trembled on my arms. "What is that ghastly noise?"

"Let her go!" Austin shouted, his footsteps heavy on the timbers. "Let her go, Uncle Nevin!"

"Go back, Austin. This has nothing to do with you. No harm has come to the child." Nevin looked at his sisters. "Tell him to go back, Delia. This must stay in the family. You promised, remember?"

"Not anymore. I can't carry that any longer." Delia Squires walked slowly down the center of the bridge and stood beside Austin with the rain pelting her face. "You killed that little girl just as surely as if you pushed her over the side."

"That's not true! You're just saying that because you liked her, played together all the time. She was trash, Adelia, common Scoggins trash!" Nevin turned and stepped backward, pushing me until the girder cut into my back.

"Amanda was your cousin, your own flesh and blood, and you hated her because Grandpa took her in to live with us, and you were afraid he'd love her best!" Delia flung herself at Nevin, pounding him in her fury, and Austin took the opportunity to snatch me from his uncle's grasp. His warm, strong hand encircled my wrist, and then my waist, binding us together.

"It's about time you showed up!" I sagged, letting him support me.

His lips touched my hair. "Sorry. We had to walk about a half mile back there. A limb fell across the road."

"Delia, stop! What are you saying?" Daisy Leatherwood plodded forward cradling Will, who was now swathed from head to toe in her huge fuchsia raincoat.

Delia gave her brother a last shove, leaving him sagging, ashen-faced, against the railing. "They know about Amanda, Nevin, that she was Aunt Ada's child."

"I used to wonder about that," Austin's mother said, "but I didn't dare ask Papa!" She seemed to be seeing her brother for the first time. "I remember when Aunt Ada died; after that, poor little Amanda never looked the same. I don't think that Scoggins woman cared a thing about her. If it weren't for Goldie—"

"Grandpa brought Amanda to Willowbend," Delia said, "and sent those Scogginses packing!" A flicker of a smile crossed her face. "It was like having a sister my own age, and he brought her that toy lamb. Remember the lamb, Nevin, that day on the bridge?"

Her brother turned away, put his arms on the railing, and wept, his frail shoulders heaving. The rain slackened, but the river boiled and rolled below us, sending wisps of fog through the cracks on the bridge.

Delia Squires spoke softly. "Nevin took that lamb away from her and made her cry. He dared her to walk the railing to get it back!"

"And she did it, too. Amanda wasn't afraid like you were, Nevin, and when she reached for the lamb, you snatched it away, held it over the water...and she fell...."

She looked steadily at her brother as she spoke. "I ran screaming for Papa. He was home on leave, and I thought he could save her, I thought he could do anything! Papa tried, but it was too late, and he cried. Remember how Papa cried?"

"Stop it! I didn't mean to! You swore you'd keep the secret, never tell." Nevin Squires sounded like a middle-aged child.

"You did mean it," Delia said. "You were jealous and spiteful, and you wanted Amanda to die!"

"Don't tell Papa, please don't tell Papa!" Nevin begged as Austin led him away.

Delia stood aside to let him pass. "Papa knows, Nevin. I think he's always known. That's why he hates you so."

I took the sleeping child from Daisy's arms and followed them across the bridge. Nevin Squires would probably spend the rest of his life in an institution, and the child who had died because of him would sleep forever in the far corner of the family graveyard.

I paused at the railing and looked for a few seconds into the foaming water. I wasn't afraid anymore. Laney was gone, really gone, and life would be very different without her. As I moved away, I noticed a sudden silence. The river had stopped crying.

Gathering Will closer, I hurried after Austin. I didn't plan to wait too long at the fair.

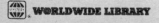

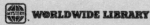